THE NIGHT YOU MURDER

Adrian Spalding

To Peter
Thank you for all your help

Adrian

OTHER TITLES BY ADRIAN SPALDING

Sleeping Malice

The Reluctant Detective

www.adrianspalding.co.uk

Acknowledgements

I often wonder if some of my friends secretly dread seeing an email from me appearing on their screen. I suspect they might, especially when the subject line is 'My new book'. Having once bravely volunteered to read my first story, they possibly never thought that they were going to find themselves dragged onto a carousel of beta reading for me. As we know once on a ride, it can be hard to get off.

Hopefully they are enjoying the ride as much as I am. Thank you to my fellow roundabout companions: Irene, Angela, Claire, Anthony, Peter, Brian and Gavan. (There are more rides planned!)

Finally, leaving the best to last, thank you to my wife, who spent hours and hours editing and making sense of my writing.

Thank you all.

CHAPTER ONE FRIDAY

Pacing anxiously around his small antiques shop, Thomas de la Mer was willing Laura to call him. He had expected that important call this morning; at the very latest by lunchtime. He looked at the Skagen watch he had bought three years ago to celebrate starting his business - it was almost four-thirty. This was not the Laura that he had once dated. That Laura was reliable, methodical and, most of all, trustworthy; today he was not sure she still possessed any of those attributes.

He had first tried calling her mobile number shortly after two o'clock, but unusually, it had gone straight to her voicemail; just as it had on the numerous occasions he had tried since. Where could she be? Was she in trouble? That last thought kept presenting itself to him. If only he knew who she had negotiated the deal with, he might be able to help. Of course, he had asked her just who the buyer was but each time she resisted, saying, 'These are shady characters; it's best you are left in the dark.' He had trusted her, so begrudgingly he had accepted what she said, even though he had handed one hundred thousand pounds to her before he watched her walk out of the shop, her perfume lingering afterwards as it always did. The real problem facing Thomas was that it was not his money, it was borrowed.

When Laura had turned up at his shop last Saturday, he had thought for a brief moment that she wanted to resume their relationship. He should have guessed that was not the reason, he was twenty years older than her; a fact she had often pointed out when they were dating. 'So why do you go out with me?' he would ask. Laura simply smiled, touched his lips with her elegant fingers

1

and told him, 'I'm an expert in ancient Mediterranean civilisations; I like old things.' He had been beguiled by her then as he still was now.

'I have the opportunity to purchase a very rare artefact, a Cycladic figurine for a very good price. I also know that I can sell it within a few days, making a substantial profit for us both,' Laura explained, 'I just need one hundred thousand pounds in cash to buy it in the first place. Knowing you like I do, I thought you might fancy investing.'

Thomas looked at her sitting on his cluttered office desk fiddling with a silver letter opener. He knew all too well he did not have that sort of spare cash, but he had contacts. He did know someone who might be willing to lend him that sort of money. The temptation of a healthy profit and impressing Laura was the driving force for him; so, he had borrowed the money and willingly handed it over to Laura. That had been the easy part.

Now he wondered, had she betrayed his trust, he hoped not. The last conversation he wanted to have was to explain how a young attractive woman had disappeared with the borrowed hundred thousand pounds. Thinking about who had lent him the money, he thought that conversation could very well be his last.

* * *

Caroline knew that it was not the best thing to do, it was just that there were very few avenues she could pursue. Laura had promised faithfully to call her earlier, and when she had not, a worried Caroline called Laura's phone. It went to voicemail, doing nothing to alleviate her concerns. An hour later Caroline tried again with the same result. Laura always responded to her voicemails, even if it was a simple text message of acknowledgement. Today here was nothing and that worried Caroline. Now it was the evening and still no word, so Caroline decided to knock at her door, see if there was a problem. She knew that Laura would not like her calling around to the house, but for Caroline these were exceptional circumstances. She pressed the white button on the door frame, heard the bell chime inside and waited.

It was not long before a man opened the door and stared at Caroline blankly, he clearly did not recognise her. They had only met a couple of times last year, she thought she might have put on a little weight since then, but not that much she hoped. Maybe he was just bad at recalling faces.

"You must be Robert." she stated, in a solemn voice.

"Yes," he sounded unsure of who she might be and what she wanted.

"You don't remember me, do you? I'm Caroline Stone, Laura's friend. She was staying at my flat when you two first met. You were visiting your friend Andy; who lives on the floor below me. When you and Laura had a problem with the lift," she reminded him.

His expression softened, "I'm sorry, of course, Caroline; I have a terrible memory for faces. What can I do for you?"

"Is Laura in?"

His face once again changed; this time a sad, anxious expression washed across it. "Ah, that is a bit of a difficult story, best if you come inside for a while." He gestured for her to enter.

The house was a pre-war semi-detached one, typical of many that lined the residential streets of Sidcup in south London. She followed him through the hallway turning right into the living area, where Robert offered her a place on the long couch that stretched from the door to the window. Caroline sat in what she thought must have been originally two rooms that had been knocked into one large room; a throwback from the 'eighties' fashion. She knew that Robert had lived here all his life, staying in the house after his parents had died. Laura had described to her how Robert, once his parents were gone, gutted the house totally, creating a modern, bright living space with clean lines. The house now had a new kitchen, new bathroom, freshly plastered walls, plus the gardens, both front and back, were professionally landscaped. Then there was his immense vinyl record collection that Laura had often mentioned. Caroline sat opposite the shelves that contained the vast number of records which resembled multi-coloured wallpaper, until you were close to them. The rest of the room was sparsely furnished, it appeared to be a room designed solely for relaxing in while you listened to music playing.

"Is something wrong?" Caroline asked.

Robert sat at the opposite end of the couch facing her, he looked sad. "I'm not sure exactly how to explain this, or where to start knowing that you are her friend, so I'll be blunt. She has left me."

"Left you?" Caroline repeated for no better reason than she was surprised at the admission.

"I'm not sure how close a friend you are to her, I don't recall her mentioning you in a while, but we were not getting on that well. She might have put a brave face on it for her friends, but things were not as they had been when she first moved in. Things got a bit heavy last night and she told me she was leaving me. She walked out last evening. Put her coat on and shouted at me that she has someone else 'who cares for her more than I ever did'. Who he might be, I have no idea; it was a complete surprise to me. Has she spoken to you about anyone else at all?"

In that moment Caroline felt sorry for Robert. They were all a similar age, Robert, she recalled, was thirty-four, a year older than Laura and her, yet he now had the expression of a little boy who had broken his favourite toy.

"She never mentioned anything to me. I've tried calling her today; I'm still waiting to hear back from her, hence the reason

4

I am here. Didn't she say where she was going or anything about who this other person might be?"

"No, I guess she was just angry when she walked out last night. I would imagine that she will, once she has calmed down, come back here at some point to collect the rest of her things."

Caroline tried to think clearly. If Laura had left Robert after an argument, then Caroline would have thought Laura would have been knocking at her door to bed down for a night or two. That was what had happened when Laura had left her parent's house. The two girls shared the cramped flat for almost a month, before she moved out so that she could live with Robert. Since then the two girls had been in regular contact. They were special friends having been through many troubled times together. Caroline should have been the first person that Laura contacted, of that she was sure.

"I'm worried Robert, truly worried that something might have happened to her."

"Sorry, I'm so impolite; all this has really put me off kilter. Can I get you anything to drink?"

"No, I'm fine, thanks. Did she take her car, her laptop, that sort of thing?"

Robert looked vaguely around the room as if he was looking for her car parked somewhere inside it.

"Of course, her car is gone, that's what she drove off in," Robert sounded a little irritated.

Caroline pointed towards the underneath of the glass coffee table that was in front of them.

"That's her laptop. Can we take a look; see if there are any clues there?"

"What good will that do?"

"I don't know, emails, messages, something. Does she do online banking that might tell us if she has used her credit card today?"

"Look Caroline, I'm sure you are concerned but she has left me, she's not missing without a trace. She more than likely is safe in the arms of her new man."

"Don't say that," Caroline snapped.

"I'm just facing facts. Sometimes you just have to accept the inevitable and move on."

"She would have called me, I know she would, and as she hasn't, I'm worried. So, can we please look at the laptop?" Caroline could hear the anxiety rising in her voice.

Robert exhaled, picked up the laptop and opened it. Sitting together on the white leather settee, he powered the laptop up. He tried to log on as Laura, but every time he entered her details the laptop refused to let him in stating the password was wrong. He tried three times. He looked frustrated.

"That is her password, I know that. Unless she has changed it and why would she change it, she must have something to hide. This is all planned, I'm sure. As I said she will have to collect the rest of her stuff sometime, including this laptop."

Caroline did not share his optimism; she had a feeling of foreboding. She was sure something untoward had befallen Laura; she just needed to convince Robert that they should find out just what had happened to her. Again, Caroline explained how Laura should have called her today, she told him that Laura had been acting strangely over the last few days, a little out of character, and she seemed to be worrying about something. Robert nodded as Caroline continued to explain they should try and discover what Laura had been doing over the last few days that might give a clue to where she is. Caroline reluctantly decided it was time to give Robert a little more information.

"I know she visited two addresses last week, both have some sort of connection to antique shops. Maybe they have some nugget of information which could provide a clue to her whereabouts."

"Why would she tell you where she visited, that seems odd."

Caroline had not planned to tell him the exact reason she knew some of the things that Laura was up to last week, but it seemed to her that Robert needed convincing that Laura could be in trouble.

"I don't really know why she mentioned the two addresses, we had just been talking about antiques and she said she was going to these two places to talk about some antique she was going to buy or sell, I can't recall which."

"She was clearly up to something behind my back. You're only confirming what I think already, this is all part of a bigger plan to move in with someone else. Do you know what she was buying or selling?"

"No. But I'm sure something has happened to her, it's just not like her not to return my calls. We need to go to the addresses."

"What you need to do is calm down, Caroline. If you take a breather, you'll see that you're exaggerating everything. The chances are that at one of those places she will be with her lover, so I'm not going to walk in on them; that would be just like rubbing salt into my wound. I'd rather not know what she is up to."

"Calm down!" Caroline threw her arms up into the air, frustrated at what she was hearing from Robert. "Have you never had someone just walk out of your life, no goodbye, no explanation, you just wake up one day and they are not there, because that has happened to me and there is not one day that I don't think of that person, wondering what drove them out of my life. I fear the same thing is happening with Laura, I need to, and I have to, know what has happened to her."

"I don't know what happened to you before, but the difference for you this time is that I can tell you, she has found another man."

Caroline ignored him, "Unless we know who he is and where she is, we should report her as a missing person to the police."

"The police!" Robert exclaimed. "What would they do, she's not a vulnerable adult, they might make a record of it, but I doubt they would do very much."

"But I have to do something; I can't just sit around and wait."

"I know you mean well but you must understand Caroline that sometimes relationships come to an end. Both parties have to step back, regroup, and then move on with their separate lives."

"Don't be so patronising, I know relationships do not always go according to plan. But I also know, call it women's instinct or whatever you want, but I just know something has happened to Laura and I want to find out exactly what that is. So, I'm going tomorrow to ask questions at the shops I have mentioned, they are my starting point; who knows what they might be able to tell me. And if they can't help, then whatever you say, I'm going to the police, I'm sure they would at least try to find her."

Robert closed the laptop down, stood up and walked across the room still holding it. He turned, standing in front of his record collection, and looked down at Caroline. She could see for the first time what Laura had often mentioned, his ears were a little too big for the size of his face. He looked at Caroline as if he was thinking, trying to come to a decision.

"Look Caroline, I get that you are worried, I get that you're concerned. So OK, I'll come with you to help put your mind at rest. But, when we find her shacked up with some bloke, then I will not be happy. Give me the first address and I'll meet you there in the morning, then we will try the second one. Remember, I'm doing this for you, because you are clearly worried and concerned for Laura, which as a friend you would be. But let's be clear I no longer care for Laura; she has betrayed me and she is now in my

8

past. Plus, if she starts having a go at me for trying to track her down, I'll point in your direction for an explanation, alright."

Caroline did not care; the important thing was that she was doing something.

FRIDAY ONE WEEK EARLIER

Laura had never met Gerald Wallace, but she recognised his type; in fact, she knew an awful lot about him. She had been able to gather plenty of useful information, which would enable her to force him into a corner from where he would have no choice but to give her what she wanted, a name; confirmation of what she suspected. Then she would leave this rich, dirty old man alone.

He had warmly welcomed Laura into his four storey Georgian Town house, located in a fashionable part of London, without any sort of question as to who she might be or what she might want. She knew that being in her thirties and attractive would be as good as a door key. Gerald, now in his fifties, liked the company of younger women, most of whom, Laura knew, he had to pay for.

"I'll try and take up as little of your valuable time as I can, Mr Wallace," she lied.

"Please feel free to take as long as you want, Miss, it is not often that I am visited by such an attractive, young lady. Can I get you a drink?"

She refused the offer as they both sat down in separate green leather, wing-backed Chesterfield chairs, both of which had seen better days. The whole room was from another era. The high ceiling was decorated with painted-plaster frescos. Dark, heavy damask curtains framed the large sash-corded windows. Faded patterned wallpaper covered the walls, which were largely covered by several large oil paintings; nothing famous, Laura concluded. Although she was impressed with the large piano that stood close to the tall bay window that

9

overlooked Lennox Gardens. She nodded towards the grand black ebony piano.

"A New York model M about 1927?" Laura knew antiques. Gerald shrugged his shoulders; she guessed to him it was just a piano.

"Came with the house when I inherited the whole lot from Daddy, it gives the cleaner something to focus on. So, have you come to buy the piano or is there something else you want to talk to me about?"

Laura smiled, he seemed incredibly relaxed; she knew that was about to change. She took from her handbag an envelope and looked at the typed name and address.

"This, I believe, is addressed to you," she recited the name and address.

"I wish all post office workers were as attractive as you." He leaned forward to take the letter, which Laura snatched out of his reach.

"Not so fast, Mr Wallace, or can I call you Gerald. Inside this letter is an odd piece of plain white paper with the words: 'Hurrell Services Facility Management (HRSR). 30,000'. Unusual sort of correspondence, don't you think?"

Leaning back into the cracked leather of his chair, Gerald replied, "I think personal correspondence is private; a private affair between two people, in this case, you are neither of them."

"Maybe, but I do know one of the people, you. Your name is on the outside of the envelope and that is one clue. I just want to know who the sender of this cryptic message is."

"As I mentioned, young lady, it is a private matter," Gerald's face was no longer as inviting or warm.

"Let me put it another way. I think this could be connected to insider share dealing; someone giving you a tip as to a share that might be going up in price; a chance to make some serious money. That is not the way the stock market works. People who do that sort of thing get to see the inside of a police station. So, who is giving you the information?"

"I think this conversation has reached its conclusion, and it is now time you left."

Laura cautiously folded the letter and placed it carefully in her handbag. She looked at Gerald, who now appeared very nervous, maybe there was even a trace of perspiration on his wrinkled forehead.

"The conversation is over when I say it is over, Mr Wallace, and not a moment sooner. In the spirit of goodwill, I would like to share some information with you that might encourage you to share the name of the sender."

Laura spoke with a confidence that unnerved Gerald as he listened to her. She started with the simple fact that Gerald had worked for many years in the finance industry around the City of London. He had worked with investment banks, some of the best and well known, until in 2015 when he was caught accepting insider information and profiting from it. A minimal six month suspended sentence was the slap on the wrist; the banning from ever working again in the City was the real punishment. Luckily for Gerald, he had made a small fortune from his City career to fall back on. This allowed him to spend more time taking recreational drugs and employing the services of high-class escorts, which was fine for a couple of years. Then, Laura pointed out, like any other fifty-seven-year-old, the body starts to tire, and a more satisfying excitement can be found in buying shares at rock bottom prices and seeing them rocket in value. Laura could see she was having an effect on Gerald as he stood up and walked over to a small mahogany table and poured himself a whiskey. She remained silent as he lifted the glass to his lips and swallowed the large measure in one go.

"Hearsay," was his only comment.

"No Gerald, you know full well none of what I have told you is rumour or gossip, you have a criminal record; you are barred, you have some wild parties here and you are still insider dealing, so who is giving you the information?"

Gerald remained standing beside the table, holding a now empty glass.

"Just who are you, young lady? Because if you were from the police, then I am sure I would be down at the station giving a statement. If you were from the financial authorities, then I would be answering *these questions in some anonymous glass tower in the City. But sitting here in my lounge, I am wondering if you are some sort of jealous freelancer who wants a piece of the action I am getting."*

"If I was a jealous freelancer like you say, then when I inform both the police and the financial authorities of what you are up to, you'll see that you were wrong. But I prefer to have just the name of the person who is sharing the information with you."

"I have no plans to share anything with you." Gerald turned around, picked up the cut-glass decanter and poured himself another whiskey.

It was then that Laura saw it; a small simple figurine, lying flat on its back, keeping a small pile of paper napkins in place. There was no disguising the exaggerated curve of the top of the head, prominent nose, and wide shoulders. It looked very like a Cycladic sculpture, made around two thousand years before Christ was born. Laura needed to get closer to it, confirm her suspicions. Be casual, she thought, contain your excitement. She had studied early civilisations across the Mediterranean for many years; it was her own specialist subject. She had seen pictures in books of these figurines from the Greek Cycladic islands, even a few with just glass between her and the figure. She had held many common examples. Here she had the chance to touch a very valuable, rare example. Laura stood and casually walked towards Gerald.

"Drinking will not help; it will only addle your already drug-damaged brain cells. Just his or her name, that's all I'm asking for and you'll have the letter and I will be gone."

She now stood close to him beside the drinks table and looked down at the artefact. There were the folded arms and the deep groove between the legs, sadly minus the feet that would have pointed downwards. Laura was convinced she was looking down at a Cycladic marble figure from the islands of the Aegean Sea, made over four thousand years ago. She looked at Gerald; he had no idea exactly what he had neighbouring his decanter.

"That's an unusual napkin holder." Her heart raced. She picked it up, held it as casually as she could in her now clammy hand.

"That thing, some of the old 'tut' that my father left me when he died; rooms full of rubbish and a crumbling house in the country and this place, not much of an inheritance."

Laura put back the figurine gently on to the napkins. Making up her mind, she looked at Gerald and said,

"Well if you're not going to give me the name today, I will go now, give you some time to think things over. You can expect to see me again very soon."

She turned and walked out of the house without another word being exchanged between them. She knew she would come back and she knew that next time that valuable figure, which would change her life, was, one way or another, leaving with her.

CHAPTER TWO SATURDAY

"Laura has not had any work from that insurance company for at least three weeks, so why would she visit an antique shop in her own time?" Robert asked as they crossed Sloane Square.

Caroline considered his question stupid. Robert had lived with Laura for over a year and still he had not picked up on just how enthused she was about anything more than one hundred years old. Caroline knew full well that Laura's idea of a good day out would be touring second-hand shops examining unfamiliar objects, searching out gems within the detritus of house clearances. She would then follow-up with a few hours looking through antique shops, just to be amongst old belongings, and adding to her knowledge.

The shop was small and a little cramped; it occupied a tiny part of Symons Street in the shadow of a large department store. Once they were inside, the smell of wood polish was exceptionally strong. Most of the stock was of dark furniture, which Caroline considered to be opulent and not functional for everyday living. The low ceiling did nothing to help the claustrophobic feel of the shop. Caroline moved between the cabinets, chairs and tables, thinking she had been in better laid out second-hand shops.

"Good morning to you both, can I be of any assistance to you?"

Caroline turned to her right to see a man dressed in a brown herringbone jacket, white open-necked shirt, Levi jeans and brown brogue shoes. He was in his fifties, of slender build and a little taller than her. It was his accent that perplexed Caroline, it was some sort of regional mix that she could not quite identify, although she did recall a similar accent from someone she had once worked with but could not recollect who.

"A young lady came here last week, a friend of ours, Laura. She has gone missing and we wondered if you might be able to help?" Caroline asked bluntly

"I've known a lot of Lauras in my time, none of which are in the shop at present. So, unless your friend is hiding somewhere, it's just the three of us here. Could you be more precise about who she might be or look like, that would be helpful." There was, Caroline thought, a tone of sarcasm in his voice, and something else within his words that she could not quite understand.

Robert took his time to give a description of Laura, which Caroline thought was very precise, clearly, he knew more about her looks than her interests. He also shared the information that Caroline had given him, that it was sometime over the last week or even earlier this week, and that, no doubt, she would have asked lots of questions about the furniture on display.

"Yes, now that does ring a vague bell, but nothing very memorable," the man in the shop answered in his unusual twang.

Caroline looked at him, she too was having a moment of recognition. As he continued describing how someone fitting that description did come in earlier during the week asking about the Chippendale furniture that he had on display, Caroline started to reflect where she might know him or his accent from. Antiques, a lot of old furniture around the shop, a posh-sounding voice that did not sound genuine, now she remembered it from her six months working as a receptionist at the London Auction House.

"You're Thomas de la Mer, aren't you?"

A worried look washed over his face. "Do I know you?"

Caroline did not answer his question; instead she asked one of her own, "Didn't you date Laura many years ago?"

Robert turned to Caroline, a surprised look on his face, but before he could speak Caroline carried on.

"Laura once spoke of an ex-boyfriend who had a big interest in Chippendale, the furniture guy. I recall your name for the simple reason it is half French, Thomas de la Mer, Thomas of the sea. Laura said the only French inside you was Bordeaux wine."

Thomas's face flicked between the two people standing in front of him with a look of having been caught with his hand in the biscuit barrel. He hesitated, and then said,

"Laura, oh that was a few years ago now," he paused, then continued with more confidence, "Well yes, she did come in earlier this week, I just assumed you were talking about another Laura, couldn't imagine my Laura going missing." Thomas smiled, "So, how come you know Laura?"

"I used to work with her," Caroline answered, "and you, at the London Auction House. This is Robert, her partner." Thomas appeared to be confused, he was about to speak when Robert butted in.

"So just what was your ex-girlfriend doing here?" Robert asked, with a tone of jealousy. Caroline could imagine what was going through his mind. Thomas was clearly a likely candidate for the other man in Robert's eyes.

"She was just passing by, apparently she heard that I had invested my life savings in this little shop and wanted to see how things were going. She stayed maybe an hour, we chatted, had a coffee and then she left. So, you're now saying that she has gone missing?"

Caroline could see that Thomas was keen to avoid any further questions about his relationship with Laura, which she thought, in view of Robert glaring at him, was a very wise move on his behalf.

"She walked out on me Thursday night," Robert spoke sternly, "I think she was seeing someone else, and no doubt she is with them now." The accusation that he was making was obvious to Caroline and she guessed to Thomas, who had failed to divert the line of questioning.

"Nothing else?" Caroline interrupted, "no mention of going away, meeting again, anything she might have wanted to ask you about antiques?"

Shaking his head, Thomas said sorry. Referring to Roberts's obvious accusation, he explained that he and Laura had met a few years ago when they both worked at a London auction house. They had a couple of dinners out, but that was all, they were both more interested in old relics than in each other.

Caroline left her telephone number with him, in case Laura should happen to pop in again, Thomas promised he would call if he had any news.

As they crossed back over Sloane Square to the underground station, Caroline said that she did not believe a word Thomas had said. She also added that although he was an ex-boyfriend of Laura's, she knew that Laura hated him and would never go out with him again. She hoped to deflect what Robert wanted to say.

He said it anyway, "She would not be the first person to go out and rekindle a relationship with an ex-boyfriend. You seem to know a lot about Laura and what she thinks and does."

Robert asked as they sat side by side on the underground train, which was rattling its way towards Hammersmith station and their next address, "Just how did you and Laura become friends?"

"It was not that long ago actually, just a couple of years. I was working at a restaurant, well more like an up-market café in Lewisham. I was the one going around taking orders, serving, clearing tables, a waitress, it was a job, reasonable pay and good tips. As I recall it was a Tuesday, not that that's important, but it was my first day back from a long weekend away.

"Laura was reading a newspaper; there was a picture of three coffins draped in the British flag, they were soldiers killed in some sort of helicopter crash. My father served in the forces, so I could understand what those families might be going through. As I put her meal in front of her, I passed a sympathetic comment. 'A tragedy for the families,' she replied, 'maybe sad but also lucky'. Well I wasn't too sure what to make of that, but then she started sobbing. Well, of course, I comforted her, and since then we have been friends. Although she has never really quite explained just why she burst into tears, not that I haven't tried to bring up the subject, but I have never pushed her about it, I was just sure she would tell me eventually."

"But you just said to Thomas you knew him and Caroline from working at the London Auction House."

"That was after my spell as a waitress. I was just a lowly receptionist, I never spoke to Thomas, but knew of him. It was just an odd coincidence that I ended up there. I recalled Laura from the cafe, yet she did not recollect speaking to me in the cafe. There were lots of auction house staff and I was not one of the elite experts, I just answered the telephone and greeted visitors. Laura and I did became friends, and you know how girls chat, that was when I learned she had dated Thomas for a few weeks."

They had expected the next address, close to the Barnes Wetland Centre, to be another shop of some description. In fact, it was a residential house, a large double-fronted detached house. There were no cars on the weed-less gravel drive, the bay windows, edged with wisteria, were shuttered and closed. They rang the bell and waited. Nothing, no one answered, the house was unoccupied. The garden was well-tended, with beds of colourful flowers and a low hedge which bordered the frontage. Were the owners out shopping, or on holiday, there was no knowing. They left; a moping Robert to return to his own house and a worried Caroline, who told him she would return to Barnes either later that day or in the morning. Robert shrugged his shoulders and left Caroline at the tube station.

* * *

Sheila Jenkins adjusted the grey blanket, tucking it around her husband's legs.

"Stop you getting a draft," she told him.

He sat silently in his wheelchair looking beyond his wife to the street. His eyes squinted, unused to the sunshine. Sheila liked to get her husband out into the fresh air as much as possible. She preferred to put him onto the grass that they had at the front of the house as, she reasoned, from there he could watch the pedestrians passing by, be seen by the neighbours, as well as look at the cars, as few as there might be in their residential side street. He used to love cars; she hoped he was happy sitting there.

In fact, he had loved pottering around in the garden until his stroke. The minor one they accepted, he could still walk, still talk, still smile, even though it was a little lopsided. Then in the year of the London Olympics, while they were watching the rowers fight their way to Olympic gold, he collapsed. A major stroke left him unable to walk, talk, or even eat food properly, let alone smile.

"Now you sit there quietly. You'll see Teresa and Doug from number nineteen have a new car, shiny blue thing, looks very expensive. They were going shopping so will be back soon, I'm sure you'll love it when you see it."

He just stared into the distance beyond his wife.

"I'm going to do a bit of weeding while the weather is fine. They have forecast rain tomorrow, so today will be the best day."

Sheila never waited for a reply; she was never going to get any response from her husband ever again. He was sixty-one, seven years older than her. They had married when she was twenty, a young bride looking forward to a wonderful marriage, children and years of love. There were never any children, they never knew just why. They did not want to investigate to find out which one of them might be at fault, but instead they set about

19

enjoying their marriage. They had lived in various flats which they rented until they finally were able to take on a mortgage. After ten years living in a two up–two down terraced house, they finally moved into their current dream semi-detached house which they loved so much. Five years later the major stroke took the man that Sheila married away from her.

Kneeling on her gardening cushion digging out the weeds, she heard a car stop on the next driveway. She rarely saw Robert; he always seemed to be at work. Laura had moved in with him last year, she often popped in and 'babysat hubby' while Sheila went shopping or just got away for a couple of hours respite. She had seen Laura on Thursday, after that she had seen neither of them, which was not what she had expected to happen.

"Hello Robert, how are things?" She got to her feet, pulling off her gardening gloves.

"Fine thanks," Robert answered as he took his door keys from his pocket.

"I haven't seen Laura recently; even her car is not on the drive. Is she alright; not ill, I hope?"

Robert stopped and walked over to her. Sheila thought he looked concerned, not the attractive carefree young man he normally seemed.

"I'm sorry to have to tell you this, Sheila, but Laura has left me." He went on to briefly explain how things had not been going well recently and that she had walked out on Thursday night.

Sheila listened; she knew that Robert was someone who did not easily talk about their emotions. She had never really thought about whether they were getting on or not. She had known Robert for several years now. When Sheila and her husband had first moved in next door to Robert, he was caring for his mother in the house, the same house that Robert had lived in all his life. When his mother died, Robert stayed on in the house alone until Laura moved in.

"How terrible for you; I only saw her on Thursday. She had popped in for a cup of tea, and I had no need to go shopping as Tesco had delivered for me. I just popped out to the corner shop for a walk more than anything and bought some chocolate mints from that nice young man in the shop. I thought Laura just wanted a chat, well we did chat, but she never mentioned anything which even hinted that she was planning to leave you. Just women's gossip over a cup of tea and then she went home. What a shock for you. So, you don't know exactly where she has gone?" Sheila asked then added, "Or how she was feeling when she left?"

"I have no idea, I guess she was angry." He shrugged his shoulders.

"So, you're now on your own, you both seemed so well matched. Look, come around one evening, I'll cook you a meal, a bit of 'motherly love', I'm sure that will help."

"Thanks Sheila, I might take you up on that later in the week, but for now I'm OK."

Sheila watched him enter his house, and then returned to her weeding with only a quick casual glance towards her husband, who sat looking into the distance without seeing anything. Sheila wondered just why life never goes exactly to plan. Some things never go quite right, yet they always seem to work out in the end. She turned and looked at her husband; it wasn't his fault he had the stroke, she thought. But it was now down to her to make things better, something she had already begun to do.

SATURDAY ONE WEEK EARLIER

"Laura, to what do I owe this unexpected pleasure?" Thomas de la Mer hugged Laura as soon as she walked into his shop, kissed her

socially on the cheeks and then beamed at her. "Lovely to see you after, how long is it, five years?" he asked.

"More like six years, as I recall. So, this is very swish, antiques shop in the posh part of town, plus lots of that Chippendale rubbish you love so much."

Thomas recalled the time when he worked alongside Laura at the same auction house. He was the expert everyone went to when they had a piece of Chippendale furniture to identify, and Thomas liked that. At the same time, Laura worked in the ancient antiquities department; she could tell you a lot about those ancient Greeks. He liked to call her a 'Greek Geek'; she called him a 'Faux Frenchie'. He warmed to her and they had dated a number of times, before she gently hinted that he was not her type, leaving him disappointed, he liked her a lot.

"So, when did you buy this place? The last I heard you had been kicked out of your job, all very hush hush."

"I didn't fit in with the management; you know that, always trying to put me down because I never went to university only taught myself all there is to know about Thomas Chippendale. So, I left, under a bit of pressure I'll admit. Then I spent my life savings buying this place, I've been here three years now."

Laura laughed, "Life savings, you? Come on you're having a laugh Tommy. You never had any money of your own."

"I told you, I am a modest person, I never flaunted what I had; that would have antagonised the management even more."

"Well if I had known that, I might well have dated you more than a few times," Laura smiled, brushing her hair back from her face.

"Well, I'm free and single still if you want to take up again. Don't tell me, that's why you're here?"

"You should be so lucky, although money and profit are something I have come to talk about."

Thomas listened to Laura, he liked her voice; it had a tone of constant enthusiasm, which is how he would have described her. Her shoulder-length brown hair moved as she spoke. Sitting opposite each other on Chippendale dining chairs, he could smell her perfume. He hoped she was not in a relationship of any description, and he had the chance to, maybe, start dating her again. He was no longer the odd fellow who loved dark wood furniture, which was how his colleagues described him. He was now a shop owner, dealing in quality vintage furniture.

"It is an opportunity to make a healthy profit within a few days," is how Laura started, "I have the opportunity to buy a small figurine, dating from about four thousand years ago, an original made on one of the Greek islands. It's called a Cycladic marble figure. I could go into more detail, but your eyes will only glaze over with boredom. That's what happens when you study a Yorkshire furniture maker," she laughed, before continuing outlining her offer.

"Now the seller does not really want the figure, so is happy to take a really low price for it. I already have a buyer in mind, so within days, we will have made the sale and be sitting on a very nice profit."

"You're saying we, as in you and me?" Thomas asked.

"Well, I don't have enough money to buy it in the first place, so I need a partner to help me buy it and I thought of you."

'Partner', Thomas liked the way that sounded; he knew he was already almost sold on the idea; she always had that effect on him; he always wanted to please and trust her. "So how much money are we talking about here?"

"One hundred thousand."

"Pounds?"

"No Shekels, what do you think?"

"I don't have that sort of money around to hand; everything I have is tied up in this shop."

"Shame, the buyer I have in mind will be paying three hundred thousand pounds for it, so that is one hundred thousand pounds each for less than a week's work. Is there no way you can get hold of that sort of money in cash? Perhaps from the, how shall I put it, add-on business that you have running here."

Thomas frowned; she could not know about the profitable side-line that he had, could she? It was always very discreet; his special customers did not just walk in off the street and get served; they had to come recommended by other clients.

"What are you talking about?" he questioned her, wanting to know what more she might know.

"Come on, Thomas, I know lots about you, more than you would imagine. Do you honestly think I would just walk in and ask someone I knew years ago to help me out with a business deal? I always do research."

He considered her words, she was bluffing, trying to trick him. If she actually knew what he was operating from the shop, she would have just said it out loud.

"I think you are mistaken Laura, this is just a simple antiques shop, nothing complicated about that. So, I think you had best look back at your research notes to see where you went wrong."

This time Laura smiled, "I think it is your memory that is playing the tricks. I'll give you an example; didn't you just tell me you left the auction house under pressure? Well, I know the 'pressure' came from the two policemen taking you out of the building, putting you in front of the courts and they in turn sending you down for eighteen months. Although with good behaviour you were out in twelve. So, do you still think my research is rubbish?"

Thomas felt weak in the knees, even though he was sitting down. She knew about his stay in prison, so she would no doubt know the reason why, it was public knowledge if you looked in the right places. Of course, the profitable side-line that he ran from the shop was not public knowledge. She still could be guessing, fishing, hoping to catch him out, get him to admit what he does. Thomas did not want to fall into any trap she was laying for him.

Thomas remained silent as he ran the figures in his mind. It was an obvious deal, a large profit in a short time, but he really did not have that sort of money available. There was a possible way, he thought. Thomas had contacts, not exactly ethical businessmen, but people who might well lend him that sort of money. Plus, this was Laura; she had always been shrewd, which she had clearly shown him today. The overriding influence in the mind of Thomas, however, was he still fancied her.

"You really think that there is two hundred thousand pounds profit in this transaction?"

Laura just nodded.

"Look, I maybe can get hold of that sort of money, but the person I am thinking of is not exactly totally legal and above board. So, he is going to ask for a lot of interest for lending that amount of money, even if it is only for a short time."

"That's your side of the deal, in the end, I get one hundred thousand, you get one hundred thousand, if you have expenses then that is your problem."

"Yes, but I'm putting up the capital," he countered.

"If you are borrowing the money then, to be honest, Thomas, you are not putting up the capital. Even if you were, I am still bringing it all together and I have the expertise to know what I am buying is genuine."

"OK. I'll speak to someone about borrowing the cash. I'll call you Sunday night to let you know if I have it. I just need your number."

Laura jumped up from the chair and kissed him full on the lips.

"You are not going to regret this. Though I am a little upset that you have disposed of my number. I'll give it to you again, it hasn't changed."

Thomas did have her number in his battered Filofax, but he did not want to sound too eager.

* * *

Laura Evans felt unusually nervous as she walked up the gravel drive towards the front door. The house was imposing, a large double-fronted house with bay windows on either side cloaked with Wisteria, not yet in bloom. She hoped her unplanned visit would not annoy Howard Mullins; he was not the sort of person you wanted to knowingly upset.

She had first met Howard when she worked at the London Auction House; he had been a regular customer there, buying and selling vintage artefacts of all descriptions. He was a well-respected customer, who always received special treatment from the management.

The door was opened by a large muscular man, bald headed, who she recognised as Henry, Mr Mullins's personal assistant, bodyguard, or attack dog, depending on what was required.

"My name is Laura Evans; I would like to speak to Mr Mullins."

"Sorry, Miss, Mr Mullins is not available; you'll need to make an appointment."

"I know he is in, that's his Rolls Royce Silver Shadow sitting there. Tell him Laura wants to speak to him; I'm sure he'll agree."

Henry looked at her with a distrusting eye, closed the door, not fully shutting it, leaving her on the step. She waited and a few moments later Henry was back.

"Follow me."

Laura did, up the flight of stairs to the right of the hallway, onto the first floor, and then Henry directed her through a panelled door. The room was spacious. There was a large double bed in the middle with shelves full of books covering two walls. A large bay window filled the room with light. Howard Mullins was carefully placing neatly folded clothes into a case that lay open on the large double bed; he looked up as she stood by the door.

"Do you always greet visitors in your bedroom?" she asked, her tone was sociable, playful.

"Only those special visitors who turn up unannounced when I am about to go away for the weekend."

He walked towards her and placed his hands on her shoulders, kissing her on the cheek in a fatherly way, which he was old enough to be. She did not know his exact age, but he was in his mid-sixties at least. She liked him, he had a pleasant manner about him, unless you crossed him, then things would be very different. He was short, wore thick round glasses, had a small moustache, and his receding hair was grey at the edges. He reminded Laura of Heinrich Himmler. She was not the only one; he once told her he had been bullied at school for his looks, which had earned him the nickname Heinie.

"It's good to see you Laura, it's been a few years. How long ago was it you worked at The London Auction House?"

"Almost six years since I left, or do I need to remind you, had to leave. You still trade there?"

"From time to time, I still like doing some of my deals away from the limelight of auction houses, yet they do have their place. So, to what do I owe this unexpected visit? Which I trust will not take up too much of my time, as you can see, I am about to leave for my weekend retreat by the coast."

"Where are you going?"

"Birchington in Kent, I have a small place there which I go to every weekend to escape the odours of the capital. Helps me think and gives me time to listen to Wagner. You must join me one weekend, I am sure we could have some very interesting and stimulating conversations, but that is beside the point, I am waiting to hear the reason for your visit."

Laura walked across the room and sat on the bed, bouncing as the mattress adjusted to her.

"Well, you know how I helped you with some transactions when I worked at the London Auction House. I realised then that you like a bargain and I have one for you, if you are interested."

"Go on," Howard stood at the end of the bed.

"I have for sale an item, a Cycladic figurine of the Spedos type so it is about four thousand years old and it is in good condition. It is about ten inches long, there is a hint of red pigment on the body, and the rest has disappeared with age. The feet are no longer attached but apart from that, it is a good example. Plus, I can sell it to you at a price which, if you should decide to sell it on, you would still be able to make a reasonable profit."

Howard walked to the opposite side of the bed to Laura and continued packing his case. He did not answer at once; Laura could see he was thinking. Then he looked up and spoke,

"You know as well as I do, people can get confused between the early Cycladic period and the later periods; are you sure it is Spedos and not the Dokathismata type, they have similar traits. Any idea of which island it came from?"

Laura liked Howard for the simple reason he knew his stuff. She might have a special subject, but Howard seemed to know something about everything. How he could recall facts and details always amazed her. It made him more interesting than talking to Thomas, who unless Chippendale made it, would have no idea. Laura also knew that Howard only grasped key facts, she had the specialised knowledge.

"Well it does not come with a label, it's not from a Greek souvenir shop, but I would say it comes from Naxos, they are the most common."

Howard nodded, "Can I assume that this is a little like the arrangement we had at the auction house, where some unsuspecting client comes in hoping to sell their oil painting for a fortune, and you say it's not worth as much as they might hope, so not worth risking at auction; might be better to sell it privately, and then they are directed to me. Yes, a very profitable arrangement for both of us, as I recall. So how much are you thinking of?"

Laura was going to remind him of a previous deal the two of them were involved in, which did not turn out as planned. She decided that it was more diplomatic not to mention it at this time.

"Three hundred thousand cash, no receipt or questions about the seller. It's then yours to do as you wish. I would guess you could sell it on for four hundred thousand without too much difficulty."

Howard shut the case. "Henry," he called, "my case is now ready."

They stood in silence as Henry walked into the room, picked up the case and left them, closing the door behind him. Howard walked over to the bedside table, picked up a paper pad and started to write on it. He tore off the sheet and offered it to Laura; she took it and looked at what he had written.

"Well Laura, I, of course, would want to see the figure for myself and examine it, with an expert, before I decide finally. But, on the face of it, it sounds like we have a deal, subject to my seeing it, as I said. Plus, that is the address of my house in Birchington; take it as an open invitation; I am there Saturday evening until Monday lunchtime every week. I know you think you hate Wagner, but notwithstanding that, I am sure I can convince you of his talents over a weekend. Let me know when you have the figurine."

He walked out of the bedroom, leaving Laura with a broad grin on her face.

CHAPTER THREE, SUNDAY

"There was no need to come in person; you could just as easily have phoned," Robert sounded irritated as he let Caroline into his house. Once again, he showed her into the living room with its large collection of records. Caroline recognised the music playing.

"I never took you to be a Sam Smith fan."

"Never judge a record by its cover, if you'll excuse the pun, I have varied tastes in music. So, what is so important that you have come all the way out here to tell me face to face?"

Robert lifted the tone arm off the record, parked it safely and turned to Caroline. He remained standing, Caroline thought in the hope that she might not stay too long.

"This part of South London is not exactly out in the sticks, is it? Sidcup is still part of London, you know, even though the address mentions Kent."

"Let's not split hairs. What have you found out?"

Caroline explained that she had visited the second address in Barnes that morning. Today there was someone trimming the hedges at the front, who she thought might be the owner. As it turned out, he was just the gardener going about his work. He did provide some information and she learned that there is just one person who lives in the house, a man in his sixties called Howard Mullins. He was away for the weekend and due back on Monday afternoon. Caroline had tried to ask a few more questions about Mr Mullins, none of which the gardener was keen on answering.

"And get this," she added, "he deals in all sorts of antiques and stuff. Not the shop we were expecting but as good as;

which means Laura was visiting people last week connected with antiques."

"Let me ask you a simple question, Caroline, how come you know that Laura actually visited these two addresses?"

As he spoke, he sat down in a large leather reclining chair that was strategically placed to face the two black speakers he had located on either side of the large window which looked out on to the street. Caroline did not really want to answer that question. She had hoped it would not come up, but now that it had, she decided it would be better to lie for the time being.

"I told you on Friday, we were chatting on the phone last week and I think it just came up, we both have an interest in antiques." She hoped Robert believed her, although he did not look convinced. "So, can I suggest that we both go around there tomorrow afternoon and speak to this Mr Mullins."

"Can we make it late afternoon; I do have to go to work," he was interrupted by the doorbell; with a huff, he got to his feet and left Caroline alone while he went to answer the door.

She looked around the room, it was tidy and clean everywhere; both Laura and Robert were cleaning freaks. She picked up a photograph in a chrome frame, it was of Laura and Robert in front of the Eiffel Tower, smiling, happy and contented. Next to that photograph was a frame which held two separate black and white photographs, one of a man and the other a woman. Caroline did not know who they might be and wondered if they were Robert's parents. She quickly put the frame down as the door to the room opened.

"Caroline, this is Sheila, my next-door neighbour," Robert sounded displeased to have guests.

Sheila quickly acknowledged Caroline and sat down beside her. Robert took his place again in the large reclining chair. Almost at once Sheila started to talk.

"While you were out earlier Robert, a young man called at my door, he had tried yours without success."

"I was in," he protested.

"Maybe you were out in the garden or something; he said he could not get any reply, so he called at my house, he has found Laura's handbag."

The room came alive with both shock and surprise; everyone wanted to speak at once, all wanting answers, but it was Robert who prevailed. He moved from his chair and sat between Caroline and Sheila, taking the handbag from her and examining the outside of it.

"Where did he find it?" Robert asked as he pulled back the zip to open it.

Sheila looked sheepish. "Oh, I didn't think to ask, he seemed to be in a hurry. I was so surprised, I just said, 'thank you', I didn't think to ask any questions. I am sorry, I should have at least asked him for his name. It was just that I was so flustered when he called as I had been in the middle of bathing my husband." Caroline thought that sounded odd, and that thought must have shown on her face prompting Sheila to explain, "He had a major stroke several years ago."

Robert opened the bag, then poured the contents out over the coffee table. A lipstick rolled onto the floor and her purse landed with a dull thud. Bits of paper, a hairbrush, a long shopping receipt, a tampon, three plain ball point pens and one silver Parker pen rolled across the glass-topped table. Sheila remained sitting back in her seat, while both Caroline and Robert leaned forward and started to sift the contents. To Caroline, it looked like the contents of any woman's handbag, and at once she noticed what might be missing.

"Her phone isn't here."

"Or her car keys," Robert added.

"But," Caroline went on, "her money is there in plain sight, so it was not a robbery. But no credit cards, that's weird, I would have thought a robber would have taken the cash as well. Whatever the reason is, she no longer has her handbag. Robert this does not bode well; I think something must have happened to Laura."

"Let's not jump to conclusions. I agree it does not look good, but we don't know where it was found, the circumstances," he glanced at Sheila. "Given the state Laura was in when she left on Thursday, it could be she was in her car driving along, keys in the ignition, phone beside her, but she had put her handbag on the roof of the car and then driven off, it wouldn't be the first time she has done such a thing. The last time she was lucky to be on our driveway but maybe this time she stopped for petrol and did the same thing."

Caroline understood what Robert was saying, she had done the same thing once. Luckily, she was only reversing out of a supermarket parking space when the bag slid down the windscreen where she could not miss seeing it. She then pointed out that without her handbag Laura would not get very far. Unless, Robert reminded her, Laura was with someone, the whole picture would change.

Sheila asked if the local hospitals had been checked. Robert did not take kindly to that question.

"Yes Sheila, I have, do you really think I am just sitting back doing nothing? There might be a slim chance she was involved in an accident on Thursday night, so I checked the local hospitals."

In Caroline's opinion he spoke a lot harsher than he needed to. Sheila must have felt the rebuke, Caroline thought, as the neighbour stood up saying she needed to get back to her husband. Robert did not bother to show her out.

"Maybe it is time to call the Police," Caroline suggested as she opened the handbag, looking inside to see if there were any other clues in the bag.

"If I thought it would help, I would, but they wouldn't consider her vulnerable or anything, she'd just be on their long list of missing persons."

Caroline pulled at the handbag lining; she had seen this type of bag before. One side had a zipped compartment, which just contained some packets of sugar; on the other side there was a Velcro fastening, hard to see as the lining material looked to be continuous, she drew apart the Velcro to reveal a letter, which she pulled out reading the address.

"There's a letter here to a Gerald Wallace. Do you know him?"

"No," Robert replied sharply.

Caroline opened the envelope and took out a small sheet of paper; she read out the type-written words and numbers, "Hurrell Management Services (HRSR) 30,000." She looked up at Robert, "What do you think it means?"

Robert shook his head, "I have no idea, but it was concealed in her handbag?"

"Not exactly concealed, but in a discreet pocket in the handbag. I'll Google the name," Caroline took out her phone.

She learnt that the company provided, 'high quality service to many blue-chip companies'. She also read out a news item about Hurrell Management Services, which reported that the company, a relatively minor player in the sector, had just won a large contract to service and maintain Ministry of Defence buildings across the north of England. Caroline then looked at the share history of the company.

"Get this, the day the contract was announced, the share price went up twenty-five per cent. There's no date on this letter but I guess if you bought thirty thousand shares before the announcement, then you would make a very handsome profit. Do you think Laura was involved with dodgy share dealing?"

Robert took the letter from her and examined it. He frowned, "It was in a hidden compartment?" He asked again.

Caroline nodded, "Well, not exactly a real hidden compartment like spies have, just a discreet place where ladies can put things. Unless you've used handbags over the years, Robert, you wouldn't know."

"I can't see Laura having anything to do with shares, or government contracts for that matter. I have no idea what she has been up to over the last few weeks."

"You work for the government; do you think you can ask some questions?"

"I'm a civil servant, I work for the population of the United Kingdom," he corrected her. "The Civil Service, with all its ministries and departments, is not good at answering questions even when you manage to find the right person to ask."

Caroline Googled Gerald Wallace, all she found were a famous basketball player and a bevy of men sharing the same name. "Well at least we have his address, we can go around and speak to him. We can either go before or after we visit Howard Mullins."

"I already told you, I do have a job to do. I'll join you to speak to Howard Mullins, but you can see Gerald Wallace on your own; all you will get will be a denial."

That may be, Caroline thought, but she knew just the person who could tell her a lot more about Hurrell Services and Gerald Wallace.

SUNDAY ONE WEEK EARLIER

Thomas followed Henry along the shadowy corridor, both sides were lined with original oil paintings in ornate frames, a single display light above each. Nothing famous or particularly valuable, just a collection of English painters from the nineteenth century. On a previous visit, Howard had gone to great lengths to explain to Thomas, that he viewed his weekend retreat as a place where he could indulge in his own

*personal taste. The whole of the Birchington house was Howard Mullins;
the English painters, the art deco furniture, the small collections of snuff
boxes displayed here and there throughout the house and there was the
ever-present sound of Wagner radiating from the room ahead.*

*Thomas hated visiting this house, not only was it over an hour's
drive from London, but he hated the dark, foreboding atmosphere the
house had. He knew he should have been pleased that Howard afforded
him the great privilege of being allowed to visit him during the weekend
at his retreat, but he did not feel that way.*

*"Thomas, welcome, come in and take a seat. Drink, of course
you will. Henry, get our guest a large gin and tonic; I recall that is your
poison of choice."*

*Thomas timidly sat down as if he was there for a job interview.
Once Henry had served the drink, he left the two men to their business.*

*"So, Thomas, to what do I owe this visit? Business going well I
trust?"*

*Thomas had known Howard for several years, not really friends
more business partners who met socially from time to time. Thomas
always knew he was the underdog in the relationship, but he could deal
with that, knowing that Howard had a habit of opening doors and
making things happen.*

*They had first met in Belmarsh Prison where they shared a cell,
talking for hours about antiques, including Chippendale, as well as art
deco, Wagner's music and reminiscing about the older gangs of South
London. Thomas was serving eighteen months for selling stolen goods, or
rather auctioning stolen goods, in the hallowed auction rooms of his own
employer, which with hindsight was a silly thing to do. Howard was in
the same cell doing six months for the similar crime of receiving stolen
goods, a crime he always denied. For those who knew him well, they had
no doubt he was guilty and were only surprised that he got caught.*

*"I'm here for a favour. I want to borrow some cash, not long
term, a week, ten days at most. I have the chance to buy a certain item,
which I can turn around quickly and make a few 'bob'."*

"Interesting," Howard swirled the ice around his glass, "I assumed your business was doing well; I keep an eye on my five per cent of the turnover and as I recall that is on the up and up. So, are you living beyond your means, your council house roots starting to appear above the ground?"

"The business is doing fine. You're still getting your cut of the turnover as promised, but wholesale prices are going up and that has cut into my profit. Maybe if you changed the agreement, took less, my profits would go up and I might have a little more flexibility in my finances."

"Ah well, Thomas, as I recall, when we were sharing our little room, your idea for the shop was good; it made sense, and I was more than willing to put up the money for you to buy and stock your shop. Maybe, if you had thought it through a little better, you might have realised that turnover and profit are very different animals. So, what do you want the money for and how much are you looking to borrow?"

Thomas wanted the cash but did not want to explain exactly what was being bought with it. He was not alone in not trusting Howard; there were countless stories and myths about Howard overhearing about an item for sale or being available, then stepping in and buying it, not caring about treading on others' feet and with little concern for making friends. He did not need to keep friends as, more often than not, people in his line of business needed him more than he needed them. Thomas knew, all too well, that if he mentioned a figurine that was going cheap, Howard would dig around and find out about it and take the opportunity from Thomas without a second thought.

"One hundred thousand pounds and what I am buying, who I am buying from, and who I am selling it to, is not information I plan to disclose."

Howard smiled, "Somehow I think you will never trust me; for what reason, I just cannot fathom. We spent a good few months cooped up together, sharing stories about our South London roots. Reason for a moment, everyone thinks Thomas de la Mer has ancestors in France, I have never mentioned you are a South London boy who decided on an image change. I paid out a lot of money to buy your second-hand shop and set you up. I have never mentioned that to anyone or reneged on our agreement. So how you can sit there, drinking my gin, and say you distrust me, I am frankly a little upset."

"The only time you are ever upset is when you lose out on a deal. One hundred thousand pounds for a week or so, what sort of interest will you be charging me? I'm sure we are not close enough for me to get it interest free?"

"How right you are. I give you the hundred thousand and ten days later you give me back one hundred and twenty-five thousand. I won't ask any questions as I do trust you."

"More like own the deeds to my shop and know exactly where to find me if you need to."

"Yes, there is that about it."

Henry was summoned into the room and instructed to get the cash. He was back within minutes to hand a plain, simple, black rucksack to Thomas, who looked inside.

"There are a lot of twenty-pound notes in there; I trust there is one hundred thousand."

"We keep very precise records here and Henry is incredibly honest."

"I would have thought that having your very own private bank here, in this house, might have attracted some low life who might fancy their chances."

Howard laughed, "The last person who even thought of that, ended up going to sea and never coming back. I'll see you in ten days, my good man."

CHAPTER FOUR MONDAY

Howard only saw strangers by appointment; in his line of work he was cautious about just who he let into his world. Today, he made an exception to this rule; the man and woman that Henry had shown into his study were asking about Laura. Howard also wanted to ask questions about Laura in particular, where she might be.

Howard listened to the girl whose name was Caroline, who seemed to be taking the lead in the conversation, with Robert just sitting there quietly. He found it hard to imagine Laura, knowing her as he did, could fall for someone like Robert. And he was surprised that Laura had told Caroline that she had visited him last week, he wondered just why that information might have been shared.

Although she went 'around the houses' in her explanation, it all boiled down to the simple fact that all they knew was that Laura had visited him sometime last week. They clearly had no idea of just what Laura was doing. He was surprised that they were innocent enough to actually believe he would tell them the whole truth and nothing but the truth. Howard never, even when he was under oath or under caution, told the whole truth, he felt you should always keep something back, that way, you can often maintain the high ground.

"Do you know who I am or what I do?" Howard asked. The innocence they gave out was like a breath of fresh air to him. They both shook their heads. Howard needed to tell them something, but just what, or how much, he would have to judge as the conversation developed. He considered that, as far as they were concerned, he was just an ordinary antiques dealer buying something from someone he knows. That is innocent enough, as long as he avoided talking about his clandestine work with Laura at the London Auction House.

Howard Mullins had never planned to be an expert in antiques. He had always dreamed of being an airline pilot. Aviation fascinated him; he was in awe of the physics that enabled a gigantic lump of metal to float in the sky where he wanted to be, riding that crest of incredible physics. Sadly, to be a pilot he needed qualifications, something which Howard was not adept at obtaining. He hated school and detested teachers, so he left as soon as he could. His first real job was to steal cigarettes and then sell them. He quickly promoted himself to burglary, better money for less risk of being caught. One day, he had broken into a detached house in West Wickham, a simple daytime job, ferreting around the cupboards and drawers, looking for anything of value that he could carry away in his holdall. On a G plan sideboard, he spotted what he thought was a small trinket box. It was light, it was small, it appeared to be made of silver and had a picture of nude women bathing on the top. Howard had no idea exactly what it was, but he was captivated by the beauty of what was, in fact, a snuff box. He opened it to reveal just a few odd buttons. He closed it again and sat on the floor entranced by the item which he rolled around in his fingers, examining every inch of it. That had been the day Howard fell in love with antiques. The sound of a door being unlocked had interrupted his dreamy trance. The owner was back. Howard jumped to his feet, placed the snuff box in his pocket and grabbed his holdall. He scurried out towards the rear of the house, through the kitchen, into the garden and then swiftly over the back fence into an alleyway. He ran and ran, until there was at least half a mile between him and his victim. Now in his late sixties, Howard still enjoyed collecting antiques on the wrong side of the law. Buying them cheap and selling them on, at a substantial profit, this was the way he had made a fortune.

"Well yes, Laura did visit me last week. I knew her originally when she worked at the London Auction House. I was a valuable client of theirs so received special treatment. Laura was my point of contact at the company. I had not seen her for a number of years, when she popped in and offered to sell me a small figurine. Old piece from the Greek islands dating back about four thousand years.

"We agreed a price and she was meant to come back on the, let me think..., Friday, yes, last Friday, so I could give her the money and I would have a very attractive figurine. I was surprised when I did not hear from her after she left but thought maybe she had a better offer. That happens in our industry, you hawk something around a number of dealers and go for the one who is offering the best price." Howard watched their reaction.

Caroline, he thought, looked a little plump, although her lack of height accentuated it. Her shoulder-length, dark brown hair hung straight down on either side of her face and would have benefitted from having a good few hours in the hairdressers giving it some style. Robert looked like just the sort of boy any mother would want their daughter to marry; average height, jet black hair, fashionable stubble and expensive clothes. He could still not understand why Laura was with him or why she had turned down his own invitation to spend the weekend at Birchington.

"Where did she get this figurine, you mentioned?" Robert asked. "I don't think it will have come from our house."

Howard picked up on the concerned tone in the young man's voice, it had to be a worrying time for him.

"I have no idea, she refused to tell me. As I mentioned, it is not that unusual in this line of business, people like to protect their sources. I would imagine that she has a number of contacts in the business."

"How much was she asking for this thing?" Robert asked.

"Three hundred thousand, it was a fair price." He paused, as he watched their expressions reflect surprise at the amount he was paying. "It might be she found someone who was willing to pay a little more, that I can't tell. All I know is that she agreed to sell it to me, and I heard no more from her, which given the way she has acted in the past, does surprise me. So, do you have no idea where it, or Laura, might have gone?"

"No idea whatsoever," Caroline answered, "we are just trying to cover all bases, see if anything turns up."

With Howard's encouragement, they left. They clearly had no idea where the figurine might be or where it had come from, so Howard had no more use of them at the present time.

Caroline left her address and mobile number just in case he heard anything from Laura. Howard very much doubted he would hear Laura's voice again, a fear he kept to himself. Experts often disagreed about the value of artefacts, but Howard was certain that the item Laura was selling was worth at least three times what she was asking for. Whoever was selling the item might have found out that they had been short-changed by her, and not taken too kindly to the fact.

* * *

Robert had left Caroline soon after they departed from Howard's house, in order to return to his office. They were both left wondering about the origin of the figurine that Laura was selling.

Not content to sit back, Caroline postponed her visit to Gerald, then spent the afternoon making telephone calls to as many of Laura's friends as she knew. Much of the afternoon was fruitless, until she took a call from Andy, a friend who lived in a flat below her. Andy gave her the first positive lead. Caroline had no idea what time Robert came home from work. She had tried to ring him, but there had been no answer. Now she waited in her car outside his house, hoping he would return home soon.

* * *

Sheila wiped the food from her husband's chin for the fifth time as he stubbornly tried to feed himself with ham and pea risotto. He gripped the spoon awkwardly and did not always find his mouth. Sheila would have been happier to feed him, but whenever she tried, he became angry, refusing to open his mouth, not wanting to be treated like the spoilt child his behaviour resembled. Sheila watched the rice slide, once again, down his chin. This was not the life she had planned for herself. It was purgatory, day in and day out with the constant attention he needed, the continuous cleaning and changing of the bed after little 'accidents'. There was also the lack of any form of normal conversation. The few words he could speak were mostly incoherent and always meaningless, except for the swear words, he had no problem with those.

Her friends, his friends, had gradually drifted away. Social life was not possible with a husband who cannot walk, cannot speak, cannot eat, cannot dress himself and only has two emotions: frustration and anger. It had been like a breath of fresh air when Laura had knocked on the door to explain that she had just moved in with Robert, and that he had told her that Sheila had a husband who was not that able, and so she wondered if there was anything she could do to help.

Oh, Sheila wanted to grab her, hug her, someone showing some sympathy and understanding of what it might be like to have a disabled partner. From that moment on, Sheila had an opportunity to go out on her own, go to Marks and Spencer for some clothes, or just hang around one of the many coffee shops in town reading the paper or wasting time watching people go by. Sheila had time for herself.

Laura popped in, maybe once or twice a week, giving Sheila not only time to do the things she loved, but to also have a conversation with an adult, just a simple conversation. It surprised her just how many things she had taken for granted before. Sheila also suspected that her husband liked Laura, he seemed to enjoy having a younger woman around the house from time to time.

Now Laura was gone, never coming back; it was a shame. Things had to change for the better, Sheila could see that, and hoped that her husband would understand what she was planning, as it was going to be the best outcome for everyone.

* * *

As she got out of her car, Caroline saw Robert's face change the moment he saw who it was. He did not look pleased, but Caroline did not really care. She had information which she was sure would brighten his day.

"Laura's car has been located," was all she said.

Robert looked at her with a puzzled look and took out his keys.

"Let's go inside and you can tell me more."

Once inside, this time no offer of a seat, she stood in the kitchen while Robert made himself a cup of tea, as she explained her news.

"Laura's car has been located at a station car park, I think we should go there right now, in case there is anything to indicate where Laura might have gone or might be."

First Robert sipped his tea, then asked, "You've found her car, Caroline, how does one go about locating a car in a country as big as Great Britain?"

"There are cameras all over the place nowadays, especially along main roads, they record number plates. I would imagine you could track just about anyone driving around."

Caroline watched Robert put his cup down on the worktop, lean casually against it and fold his arms. He then put another question to Caroline, which only made her feel more frustrated. She just wanted to get in a car and drive to where Laura had parked her car.

"Caroline," his voice sounded patronising, "I haven't actually asked you what you do for a living, does it have anything to do with highway cameras?"

"Don't be daft, I've just left my job as a receptionist, so technically I am between jobs. I hope you have a spare key for her car?"

"Yes, I do. I'm just more interested in how an unemployed receptionist like you managed to find Laura's white Fiat, using ANPR cameras?"

"I have a friend; I can't say too much or I will get him into trouble, but I did ask a favour of him. He has access to all the ANPR cameras that are on the road, plus certain private ones, like those you get at car parks. Through the ANPR cameras, he picked Laura's car up at a number of locations in the early hours of Friday morning. When he was unable to get any further that way, he checked the car parks in the vicinity of the last pick up point, and that led him to say, with certainty, that the car park entrance data showed Laura had driven into the car park at 2.44 in the early hours of Friday morning."

Robert returned to his tea, took a large gulp, and then resumed questioning his guest.

"So where exactly is her car parked and why do you think that it might help us find her unless, very conveniently, she left a note."

The constant wall of questions was beginning to frustrate Caroline. She had arrived eager and pleased that she had a lead, something they could follow up. When she had been told where the car was, she was about to drive directly there herself. But she thought that was not the right thing to do, she felt it right she should tell Robert, get him involved. Now she wished she had bypassed him.

She raised her voice, "Robert, what is the matter with you, your girlfriend is missing, don't you want to find out what has happened to her. I'm a friend and I, as sure as hell, do want to find her."

"I've told you before, time and time again, she has left me. When she does resurface, then we will know who, why and when. Plus, do your plans involve leaving her car there or are we bringing it back here? Because if it is the latter, when she returns from wherever she is currently, she will have a long walk home."

"Robert, please, let's go and see what, if anything, the car can tell us about where she might have gone."

"So where exactly is this station?"

Not another bloody question Caroline thought, will his interrogation ever end.

"Birchington," she snapped, "the station car park. She entered it, as I said, at 2.44 in the morning."

"She just entered it?"

"What sort of question is that? Yes, she drove in and parked, can we go now?"

Robert tutted, looked at his watch, "Well, can I at least have something to eat first, I have only just arrived home from work. The car's been there a week, so there's no need to hurry, is there."

"Alright, do what you want, I'm going anyway, give me the spare key and I'll see what I can find."

This time Robert huffed an expression of disapproval, pulled open a drawer, then took out a car key, with the Fiat logo on.

"OK, I'll drive you down and I'll grab a McDonald's on the way."

As they left the house Robert had another question for Caroline. "Your friend he has seen the car on CCTV?"

"No, they don't seem to have any cameras like that which are working and covering the car park, so we're not sure of the exact location of her car in the car park, but she definitely entered at that time. He was able to access the entry records for the car park."

"It could have been stolen and dumped there, maybe burnt out, so don't get your hopes up."

Caroline thought for a moment, all she wanted to do was get into a car and drive there, see Laura's car for herself and look inside.

"He said the car had not left the car park, and there have been no reports of any criminal damage at the car park for a while."

"Your friend seems to know an awful lot," there was a hint of sarcasm in Roberts's voice.

"He does an important job and wants to help. Shall we go to Birchington now or do you want to hang around here all night talking about my friend?"

They drove down in Robert's car towards Birchington station. The topic of tense conversation between them was exactly what had Laura been doing from the time she walked out. Robert recalled it was about ten o'clock which would mean, they both agreed, Laura had taken almost five hours to drive, what should have taken no more than an hour, to the station car park. She must have gone somewhere else before leaving her car at the station.

That was the dilemma facing them, just what did Laura do, where did she go during those hours before abandoning her car.

Laura's white Fiat 500 was parked in a dark corner of the station car park. Almost on its own, the car park was sparsely populated with cars at this time on a Monday night. It was, as expected, damage free, locked and parked neatly within the white lines of the parking bay. It did not look as if it had been dumped in a hurry but was parked sensibly in just the same way as any commuter using the station would park.

Robert looked around the driver's side of the car, Caroline the passenger side. Nothing stood out amongst the odd bits of paper, phone charger and a packet of extra strong mints. Then they checked the compact boot.

"Her case is gone," Robert said, looking into the boot which only contained a few empty shopping bags.

"She took a case?" Caroline asked.

"Yes, when she walked out, she took a weekend case with her, the type that you pull along on wheels. She must have met someone here and then gone off for a few days; just until things settle, and then I guess, she will be back for the rest of her things."

"You never mentioned it before."

"I said she left me, how much more of a breakdown of the facts do you want for Christ's sake? She took a weekend case; she was wearing jeans and trainers, a sort of 'blousy' top thing, I have no idea what it would be called, a coat, oh, and her handbag. I told you she left me; I didn't realise you wanted to know every little fact."

Robert sounded angry, which Caroline did not want; she wanted him calm and thinking logically.

"I'm sorry, it's just that I am really worried. I think we should call the police."

Robert closed the boot and offered the car keys to Caroline. His voice was now calmer,

"To be honest, I really do wonder if that is such a good idea. She was selling something that was valuable. Howard, well I'm not sure how much we can trust him, he did not seem to me to be a person who always plays by the rules. Involving the police might not be such a good idea. Let's be honest, Caroline, do we actually know what she was up to?"

Caroline did not rush to answer that question. She did know some of the things that Laura was up to, although not everything. Laura often kept things to herself. As friendly as Laura could be, she could also be, at times, very secretive. Caroline wanted to call the police, get professionals to help find Laura, she was certain that was the right thing to do. She could also understand the view that Robert was taking. Did they really know what Laura was up to or who the people were she was dealing with? The answer was a simple no.

"If you drive the Fiat, I'll meet you back at my place." Without waiting for an answer, Robert turned back to his car, leaving Caroline, not only, to find her way back, but to also pay the parking fee for Laura's car, which she was not happy about.

She was, however, pleased that she could make her own way back to Robert's house, this would give her the opportunity to stop at the Medway services and examine the glove compartment in more detail.

There were two interesting items that Caroline wanted to look at without Robert peering over her shoulder. The first was a handwritten address in Birchington, the name alongside it was Howard, but it was not written by Laura. The second was more important, it was an envelope from an estate agent, inside there were details of three flats, all in Manchester. Caroline was not interested in the flats or how many bedrooms or bathrooms they might have, it was the address the information had been sent to that held her attention.

17 St Luke's Crescent, Lavender Hill, London

All the time she had known Laura, she had never once mentioned where her parents lived. Every time the subject came up in conversation, Laura would just say it was none of Caroline's business, she did not need to know where Laura had lived before sharing her flat. All she would say, was she had left her parents' home after a disagreement. All the time the two of them had known each other, as far as Caroline knew, certainly she never admitted to visiting her parents. Yet here was an envelope addressed to Laura at an address that was not familiar to Caroline.

Caroline wanted it to be Laura's mother and fathers' house, that would be the best option, that Laura was still in touch with them and was using the address to conceal her plans from Robert. There was another thought that Caroline could not get out of her head, that the address, or who ever lived there, could be the other person in Laura's life and Robert was right. Laura was now in the arms of someone else.

"You took your time," was the only greeting she received as she stood at Roberts's door and handed back the car keys.

"I'm a slow driver," she lied. "I'll leave you to your evening, while I try and think where she might have gone before parking the car. I'll call you tomorrow."

Caroline returned to her own car. Some things she needed to keep to herself, the address was one.

MONDAY ONE WEEK EARLIER

Laura had never seen so many twenty-pound notes before, let alone stuffed into a very boring black rucksack. They were divided into packs of one thousand pounds, each pack held together with an elastic band.

"Well, you obviously didn't get these from the bank," Laura said as she began counting the well-used notes.

"It's all there you know; I wouldn't fiddle you."

She stopped counting, "Where there's money, there is temptation, I'm checking it all, Thomas."

Even though the back office at his shop was cramped and a little musty, she was determined to ensure there were exactly one hundred thousand pounds as she had requested. As she reached thirty-three thousand, she sat down in the only chair in the room, leaving Thomas standing watching over her, as the piles of money grew on the already cluttered desk. She broke the tense silence, nodding her head towards a safe that sat in a dark, dusty corner of the room.

"If you had to borrow all this money, what's the point of the safe?"

"I do have some assets; this business is not a total failure."

The silence, but for the rustle of the bank notes, continued; Laura had reached sixty-four thousand. Her heart was beating faster than it had in a while, this was a lot of money. It felt as though she had the power to do whatever she wanted. Money corrupts, that she knew all too well, but it also had the ability to heal, if you knew what you were doing and were not taken in by the intoxicating taste of it.

"So just why did you leave the auction house?" Thomas asked.

Laura stopped counting and looked up at him. As he continued to work there after she had left, she had assumed that all colleagues would know about her. There again, the company was divided into smaller parts, so maybe her leaving had not made headlines across its grapevine.

"There were rumours that I was being a little too generous with some of my customers, giving away the company profits. They were more than happy all the time I was bringing in plenty of money for them, but the minute trading got a little tough, well, they don't understand that rules on the amount of commission need to be bent a little to keep the good customers. I gave some of my special clients a good discount on the amount of commission we took from anything they sold, a bit less for the company, a little more for the customer, and, hey presto, the customer stays; it makes sense to me. As it turned out, the management didn't see things quite in that fashion."

"I thought they sacked you because you were tweaking valuations?"

"I thought you said you didn't know why I left."

Thomas smiled and shrugged his shoulders. Laura smiled back; for all his faults, his odd accent, his dubious business, she liked him. They had dated a while back, a few dinners out, once to the theatre. He was good company once you took him away from Chippendale. However, she did not regret cooling and ending the relationship, if it could be described as a relationship; he was never going to be a long-term prospect for her.

"So, what have you been doing over the last few years?"

"You ask a lot of questions."

"I am letting you walk out of here with one hundred thousand pounds, without any idea of who you are buying from or selling to. I don't even know where these transactions are taking place. I just have your word, so I think I am entitled to ask a few questions."

"I went freelance working for a number of insurance companies. I visit people's homes, look at the treasured heirlooms they are insuring and decide if the valuation is correct."

"So, you would come to my house, look at, say a Chippendale chair, I say it is worth ten grand, you agree, and it gets insured for ten grand."

"Pretty much."

"Even if there is no such chair or it's a fake. Lots of opportunity there to make a pretty penny."

"You are such a villain, is there anything honest about you."

"I'm just saying, doing that sort of work presents opportunity. We both got fired for a little skulduggery, so you and I are not so far apart. Is that what you are doing with this cash, buying something you have undervalued?"

"I told you before the less you know, the safer you'll be."

Laura counted the remainder of the money, without further questions from Thomas, who just stood looking at her nimble fingers flick through the notes. She then re-packed the money into the rucksack and kissed him on the cheek.

"Once I have bought the item, I'll pop back and show it to you before I sell it on. That will prove to you I am buying something."

Before she could turn to leave, Thomas grabbed her by the arms and pulled her towards him. He then locked his lips onto hers, giving her a passionate kiss, holding her all the time close to his body. She felt no fear, she had known him well when they worked and dated together, she knew he would let go and look a little sheepish as he stepped back from her, which he did. Laura touched his nose with her finger,

"You're still a good kisser, one day you'll make a good husband for someone. And before you ask, I'm not that someone."

Without another word she walked out of the shop into the early evening rush hour.

* * *

Arriving in the hallway of her house, Sheila placed the two shopping bags carefully on the beige carpet with its clear plastic runner running the length of the hallway.

"I'm back," she called out.

She had popped into town to collect a few bits for mid-week dinners: some fresh vegetables, sliced ham, low-fat mince and another pint of milk. Cooking for her husband was easy enough; the food needed to be easy to eat, so mince, porridge, chicken pieces and even salmon had become their staple diet. No more did they enjoy the roast dinners or steaks that they had before.

"I've put the kettle on," Laura called out from the kitchen as Sheila took off her coat and carried the shopping into the kitchen where

Laura, who had been looking after Sheila's husband, was preparing two fruit infusions.

Once the shopping had been put into the correct cupboards, Sheila sat down with her infusion and looked over her shopping receipt. Laura sat opposite and lifted the red tea bag out of her cup.

"He has been as good as gold while you were out," Laura reported. "We watched TV for a while and then we did a crossword, not that he was much help with it," Laura joked.

Sheila folded the till receipt and looked across the table, "You're so lucky to have someone in the house who can talk to you, exchange ideas, just be another complete human being."

"Well, even the complete human beings you live with can be a pain at times."

"Ah, but not Robert," Sheila was wistful as she recalled the time before Laura moved in next door. "I always found him to be a very caring person, helpful and with such a good humour. We had some great times together before you moved in."

Laura smiled, "Sounds as if you were more than just good neighbours."

"Oh, didn't he tell you?"

"Tell me what?" Laura now looked puzzled.

"Well it was before you arrived, so I don't feel guilty about anything that we did. My husband just sat in the chair; he was far from being what a husband should be to a wife. Robert visited more and more. Naturally we became very close, he was in here most days. I often cooked for him, and well, it made sense, as he was at work all day, it just seemed the right thing to do. I would make him some special meals, things my husband would not be able to eat, so I also benefited from the arrangement. In time, I guess nature took its course and we became lovers," then Sheila added quickly, "of course when he met you everything stopped, as it should."

"You and Robert had a thing going, well you crafty old girl, he never told me."

Sheila was relieved that she could not hear any jealousy in Laura's voice, it had been a difficult confession to make, but it was one that she knew she had to make. Being honest with Laura was the correct thing to do; there was no point hiding from the facts. She also knew that it would help things over the next couple of days, help to lubricate the wheels of her plan. Sheila did not recall exactly who had told her, but years ago someone did say to her, 'there will come a time when you will get fed up with looking after him; a point where you will say, why me, why am I being punished like this. At that point you have a choice, sit back and do nothing and see nothing change, or stand up straight, step firmly forward and make things change the way you want them to.'

Sheila had decided she had had enough of the sentence she had found herself serving, it was now time to break free.

CHAPTER FIVE TUESDAY

St Luke's Crescent turned out to be a long road of well-cared for terraced houses, each one with its own small front garden. As Caroline walked slowly along the road looking for number seventeen, she noticed every garden looked tidy and well-tended. The trees bordering the street had been heavily pruned leaving them as tall trunks.

Number seventeen had a low brick wall with a white plastic fence fixed on top. The wooden gate was painted red, matching the door to the house. There was a window to the left of the door and two more windows on the first floor. The front garden consisted of plain pea gravel, with a general rubbish bin and a recycling bin placed on one side of it. Caroline rang the doorbell and waited.

The man who opened the door was tall and thin, Caroline guessed him to be in his sixties. He wore thick-rimmed glasses and in his left hand he was holding a wet tea towel.

"I'm sorry to disturb you, but I'm looking for Laura Evans."

"She's not here, I'm afraid."

"But you know her?"

"Yes, she's my goddaughter, known her since she was in nappies. So why are you looking for her?"

"She hasn't been heard of since last Thursday and I was hoping you might have heard from her or be able to shed some light on what might have happened to her."

His voice changed, from soft and welcoming, to tense and concerned, "No, I too haven't heard from her for about a week or so. Please, you had better come in and tell me more."

He opened the door fully and ushered her in, asking her to excuse the tea towel, explaining he had just been catching up on his washing up. There was no hallway, the house was far too small for such a luxury, so she stepped straight into the living room, which contained a grey fabric settee and a large flat screen TV that dominated the room. He introduced himself as Tim Rowe and said that he lived alone at the house.

Caroline began, "Last week Laura left the home that she shared with her partner, took her car, a case and little else. Her handbag has turned up, but sadly we don't know where it was found. What we do know is that her phone, car keys and credit cards were missing, everything else, including some cash, appeared to still be in the handbag. We have also found her car parked at a station in Kent. It was in her car that I found the estate agent letter addressed to Caroline at this address. So, you can see why I am so concerned, it is not like her at all, we always keep in touch."

"I can see why you are worried; it sounds very mysterious. No other clues at all?"

"Nothing. Her partner, Robert, suspects that she has left him for someone else, which could be true, although I hope not. You can see when I saw your address, not knowing who lived here, I began to conjure up all manner of scenarios."

"That is understandable, but I can assure you I am just her godfather."

"So why was she using your address and not her own, didn't you think that odd?"

"Difficult question to answer," Tim pointed out, "but I'll do my best. You are Caroline, yes, Laura has talked about you a few times, all good things I can assure you. So, you'll be the first to understand that Laura kept a lot of things to herself"

He folded the tea towel neatly and placed it carefully on the corner of the coffee table. Caroline noticed a recent copy of Soldier Magazine alongside a half-eaten bar of dark chocolate and a well-worn TV remote. Tim leaned back in his chair and spoke through his hands which he held in the shape of a pyramid. Caroline noticed the thumb on his left hand was missing.

"Not sure the best place to begin in order to help you, so I will start with a little background. I served with Laura's father in Northern Ireland during 'The Troubles'. We became good friends, so when Laura was born, I was really chuffed when he asked me to be a Godfather to her, a real honour, never had anything like that before. Not that I could ever reprimand her for not going to church, as I never go, but I sort of felt a responsibility towards her. After her father and I were given our discharge, we sort of lost touch."

Caroline looked at Tim, carried out a mental calculation in her head and asked, "You were young to be discharged?"

"Yes," he held up his hand, displaying the missing thumb, "the Army like their men whole and in one piece. Her family took part in less and less regimental events and in the end, well, I haven't seen her parents in years; in fact, it was the same with Laura until about a year or eighteen months ago, I forget. She, just like you, knocked at my door; I was pleased to see her, I had not seen her since she was about ten or eleven. It was good to see that she had matured into such a beautiful woman.

"From what I gather - she was being a little cagey - she was no longer living with her parents, after some sort of argument or disagreement, and she wanted to know if I would mind her using this address so that her mother could still write to her. I, of course, asked why her mother could not send letters direct to wherever Laura was living; all she said was that it was complicated, so I said fine, happy to help. So, from that point on, letters for her arrived here and she would come over occasionally and collect them, stay for a cup of tea and a chat about old times and then she would be on her way."

Caroline tried to take in all this information and connect it up with what she already knew. She understood that Laura had been in touch recently with her mother, but she had not known that she had kept in regular touch before that.

"What about the estate agent letters?" Caroline wanted to know just how much Tim knew about the quest to find a flat in Manchester. That could well be the final clue that she was looking for. She hoped that Laura might have confided in her godfather, perhaps told him the unfettered truth.

"Not sure about those. She asked if I would mind some estate agent letters arriving for her, I, of course, said it wouldn't be any problem. She did explain that she was looking to move up north somewhere. I felt that she was finding herself in a bit of a pickle and although I asked her, she clearly did not want to share anything with me. I assumed it was all personal stuff, so I let it be. I do imagine it will be about getting away from her parents, maybe starting a new life with someone, I would fancy. So that sort of ties in with what you said earlier. I'm sure she would make a wonderful wife for some lucky man. Look, it might be better if you speak to her mother, she was always the one with the common sense. She might be able to help you in finding Laura."

Caroline left seventeen St Luke's Close with another address written on a scrap of paper; the one for Laura's parents, where Laura had spent her childhood and most of her life. Caroline had promised Laura that she would never try and contact her parents or ask any questions about just why Laura had left the family home to arrive at her flat one winter's evening with just a small suitcase, pleading with her to let her stay for a few nights. Caroline took her in without question. Now she was going to break that promise; she was doing so because she was sure Laura was somewhere and in danger.

* * *

The bungalow Caroline stood in front of had seen better days. The wooden picket fence that held back the overgrown garden was weathered and crumbling, causing it to lean over at an acute angle. The paving slabs that led up to the front door with its peeling paint, had weeds filling the joints. There was a black plastic rubbish bag dumped to one side of the door. Caroline guessed that Laura would have felt ashamed of her parent's house; perhaps that was the reason she had left. Caroline hoped she was about to find out. She pressed the doorbell, heard nothing, so waited politely for a few moments, then rattled the letter box hoping that someone would answer the door.

A short grey-haired woman answered the door. She stood with a tired posture and looked up at Caroline with anxious, watery eyes. The apron she was wearing over a floral dress was stained with the ingredients from past meals.

"Mrs Evans?"

The woman nodded to affirm that was who she was, she also mumbled something that Caroline could not understand.

"I'm trying to locate your daughter, Laura. She has walked out on her partner and I'm trying as many places as I can think of to find her. Have you seen her recently?"

The woman stepped forward, pulling the door to behind her. She spoke quietly, "No I haven't seen her since last week. Is she alright?"

"Well, I hope so, that is one of the reasons I am searching for her."

From inside the bungalow a male voice shouted out angrily, "Mother, who's at the door?"

She turned and replied, still holding on to the door, "Nothing important, dear."

"Well, get on and close the bloody door, I'm getting a draft in here."

Mrs Evans seemed nervous as she looked once more at Caroline then back into the house. Caroline guessed she was trying to make some sort of decision.

"You'd best come in for a while."

Caroline followed Laura's mother along a cluttered hallway, turning right through a doorway that had no door, just the hinges left in the frame. The sense of heat overwhelmed Caroline as she stood beside Mrs Evans and looked around the room to see a gas fire which was on full. A large flat screen television set was on, but the sound was muted. There was an Ercol colonial chair with frayed floral cushions and then sitting in a large armchair, with the integral foot stool extended, was a man. He looked ancient to Caroline, but exactly how old he was, she could not be sure, maybe in his seventies. His facial skin was full of wrinkles and had a grey tinge to it. It was the things that Caroline did not see that made her quiver. He had one leg missing completely, while the other leg ended at the knee. His left arm finished at the elbow; a rounded stump of pink skin was exposed below his short-sleeved shirt.

"Who the fuck is this?" he spat the words angrily towards Mrs Evans, "If she's another do-gooder social worker...."

"It's a friend of Laura's."

"I told you before, Mother, I don't want to hear that name in this house ever again. She is no longer our daughter," the rage in his voice continued.

"But this lady says that Laura is missing."

"I've no interest."

"Mr Evans," Caroline spoke, she was not going to stand in the room and just watch a married couple argue as she guessed they did on many occasions. "We are talking about your daughter; anything could have happened to her. She has not been in touch with anyone since last Thursday, I'm worried, and I would have thought you would be worried also."

Caroline watched as his eyes narrowed with anger, if they were a death ray, she would have been vaporised in an instant.

"Why should I worry about her, she never worried about me or my feelings? She just did whatever she wanted, when she wanted. What sort of caring daughter is that, I ask you? She walked out of this house and I have no desire to see her cross my threshold again. If she's in trouble, well it serves her right."

"Looking at you, I guess you need all the help you can get, so pissing people off is not a good strategy," Caroline regretted her words as soon as they left her lips. It was just Mr Evans seemed to be able to bring out the worst side of her with very little effort.

No wonder Laura never wanted to talk much about her parents. Every time the subject came up in their conversation, all she would say was, 'it's not guaranteed you will like your parents; in the same way, you should not feel a need to love them unconditionally. They are a different generation with different ideas and different standards. You can either live in their time slot or go out on a limb and live your own life in your own way.'

"What do young people know about anything, you're all for yourselves. Look at me, I didn't do this to myself, I suffered for someone else. So, you can piss off, young lady, and leave me in peace."

"I am guessing it was trying to keep the peace in Northern Ireland that you came by those ghastly injuries?"

He did not answer at once but stared at Caroline as she waited. A moment later he began, his voice calmer and softer.

"I joined the 'colours' when I was just a boy, doing my bit for Queen and Country. Then they sent me to Northern Ireland, for 'The Troubles', they said, little bit of civil unrest, they said. It was a fucking war, gun shots, bombs and all the time the fucking IRA were trying to kill us, on or off duty; they didn't care. I was helping out the RUC at one of their training barracks, September fourth, it was, I hadn't even seen my newly born daughter when the 'provo's' dropped three mortars into the place, one landing almost next to me. I wish it had hit me on the fucking head, then I wouldn't be sitting here like a useless man, relying on everyone else. Ever tried wiping yer arse with half a body? So, the Army saved me, only to keep down the number of deaths, make 'em look good, shipped me back home, gave me a shitty pension and left me to get on with my life. Yes, I'm pissed, why wouldn't I be?"

Caroline moved towards him, her opinion of him had changed in an instant, she was overwhelmed by sympathy. She was planning to sit on the small stool beside him, hold his hand, offer him some warmth but before she could sit down, he spoke again, his tone sharp once more.

"Don't bother sitting down, young lady, you're not staying. I don't want any friends of Laura's in my house."

"But why did she leave you?" Caroline could see he had unassailable barriers, that would not be broken down easily.

"None of your business, Miss. It's about time you left."

"You're not in the least bit worried about your daughter?"

"She's made her bed, so she has to lie in it now. I told her I didn't want the likes of her in my house anymore. I told her to get out and stay away, she was no longer part of my family. Anyway, why all the sudden interest in her, why does everyone want to know where she is? I don't care, it's time for my nap."

With that he closed his eyes, shutting out everything and everyone around him. Caroline thought he was acting like a big kid, so turned and started to walk out of the room, followed by Mrs Evans. When they got to the front door, Laura's mum apologised to Caroline.

"You must forgive him, before the attack he was a lovely man, that is why I married him. But when he returned from Northern Ireland as half a man, he couldn't show affection or even tolerance towards his daughter."

"What did he mean by everyone wants to know?"

Mrs Evans opened the door, standing beside it, she glanced back towards the room and then looked into Caroline's eyes.

"A man called yesterday, I think he might have been her boyfriend at one time, I think I recognised his face. He asked if we had seen Laura recently, he was trying to get in touch with her again. Father was just as grumpy to him as well, it's not just women he moans at. I did try and help, I gave him a recent letter that Laura had sent me; I think it was saying something about going away with someone. My eyes are not too good nowadays and I have never been able to read well. Father used to do all my reading for me, but he is not interested anymore. The young man read it all, said it might help, so he took it, in case it was."

Caroline walked away from the bungalow thinking about Laura and how living in that house would have been such a source of conflict. She could imagine Laura standing up for her mother while her father shouted her down; maybe leaving the family was for the best, for everyone. Caroline wanted to scream or punch something to dispel her anger. Why had that stupid woman given away that letter to someone she barely recognised or knew? What was wrong with her, couldn't she understand how important it might be?

* * *

Caroline sat on a wooden bench in a small patch of greenery close to Putney tube station, trying to understand the meaning of what she had learned over the last couple of days. Nothing made much sense to her. Laura seemed to be selling a figurine for a lot of money, but then had not seen through the deal she had made; had she got a better offer? Then there was the argument with Robert, just storming out with her weekend case, perhaps already packed; was it too, pre-planned? But then it appeared to all go wrong, during those missing hours. What did she do in that time? Why did she leave her car in a station car park? Did she meet someone else?

Caroline put a theory into place: Laura had spent the four hours selling to someone who had made her a better offer. After that meeting, she had met someone else in the car park, and they left together to start a new life further away, maybe Manchester as the estate agent letters showed, her godfather had said she was looking at moving north. Caroline hoped that she had not gone to Manchester as that would be just too cruel.

The letter to Gerald Wallace was going to be the key. What was Laura's connection to him? Insider share dealing, that did not sound like Laura, but if there was money to be made, then perhaps the temptation had proved too much for her. First, Caroline wanted to know more, so, once again, she called Andy Lane.

Andy lived in the same block of flats as Caroline, they were friendly neighbours and he was happy to help with a few favours when asked. His real value was the Government department he worked for. Caroline was not sure exactly what he did; what she did know was that when asked, he could find out about more or less anything. He had located Laura's car with such ease, it reeked of Big Brother. She dialled his number and waited for him to answer.

"Caroline, how are you doing?

"I need a favour, Andy."

"Straight down to business, nothing like being direct. What can I do for you?"

"I want you to find out as much as you can about a person called Gerald Wallace. I don't have any date of birth or anything, but I do have an address for him. Plus, I think he has or had a connection to shares or share dealing."

"You're right, been a bit of a naughty boy in the share dealing department has our Gerald."

"You know him?"

"No, I don't know him, but Laura asked me about him a couple of weeks ago. So, I sifted through my computers and gave her the information. If you want to hang on a second, I can give you what I gave her, I should have it here somewhere. Oh, while I've got you on the phone, tomorrow I reach the grand old age of twenty-eight, I'm having a lunchtime drink with some mates from work and some friends, I'd love you to join us. No presents required, just funny birthday cards, the funnier the better. Here we go, Gerald Wallace."

Caroline listened as Andy gave her the breakdown of what Gerald had been up to over the past few years. In addition to his business interests, she heard about the insider share dealing, the debts he had as a boy, his one marriage and one divorce. She made hurried notes as Andy spoke.

"Did Laura tell you why she wanted to know more about Mr Wallace?"

"No, and I never bothered asking, sometimes it's best not to. I'm sure she had her reasons as I am sure you do, which, I am guessing, is part of tracing Laura."

"Nothing more on her?" Caroline asked hoping against hope that he would say yes.

"No, not a peep, her credit cards have not been used since Thursday, nor her phone or passport. Nothing so far, but let's not give up hope, I'm sure she is out there somewhere safe and sound."

"Andy, you know I'm asking this for Laura's sake, but did she ask about anyone else over the last couple of weeks?"

"I've got it written down here somewhere, hold on. Yep, two blokes, Howard Mullins and a Thomas De La Mer. They have a longer list of background stuff; I'll give it to you tomorrow at the pub."

TUESDAY ONE WEEK EARLIER

The salmon, sitting on a bed of curried leeks, smelt wonderful to Robert. The new baby potatoes with tarragon butter melting over them only made his mouth water more. He would be the first to admit that, at times, Laura could be a little distant, even cold, however, her cooking skills were second to none. That was not the only reason he liked her in his life: she was good looking, had a sense of humour, and they could talk for hours about almost anything. Maybe some would say their sex life was not what it should be, but that did not worry Robert at all.

He was only eighteen years old when his world fell apart in the space of a few short weeks. The result was Robert never went to university, but instead stayed at home and looked after his mother. She was grappling with the demons in her head after discovering the body of her lifeless husband hanging from a rope attached to the stair bannister.

Robert needed to curtail all those raging hormones and desires that eighteen-year-old boys have and settle into a routine of housekeeping and caring for his mother, with her unpredictable outbursts of rage and lengthy stays in dark valleys of depression. For eight years Robert was her carer; social life and relationships were not something Robert began to experience until after he had watched his mother's coffin lowered into the ground. Even then, what love and passion he felt was directed towards his ever-growing collection of music that had been his only form of escape during the years he looked after his mother.

"What's this record you're playing?" Laura asked. "It sounds kind of Chinese." They sat opposite each other at the table eating their meal; as always, there was music playing in the background.

"Close, but no cigar, it is Vietnamese dan bau music. I picked up the album at that really tiny record shop in Soho, which always has little gems to purchase."

"Well, I think Dan, whatever his name is, could be a bit livelier with his music, although I guess it might work for an insomniac."

Robert laughed, he knew Laura preferred rock music, she was a fan of Bon Jovi and Aerosmith, so he guessed that these soft melodies were not going to float her boat.

"Dan bau is not a person, it's an instrument, a traditional Vietnamese instrument. Maybe not everyone's cup of tea, but you must admit, it does add variety to my music collection."

"Well I think it surpasses Leonard Cohen as the music of choice if you're going to commit suicide," Laura stopped abruptly. "Sorry, I didn't mean....."

Robert stopped her in her tracks, "It was a long time ago, you shouldn't have to feel like you are treading on egg-shells when you are around me." Then in a more playful tone, "Although I can play Leonard Cohen, if you prefer?"

Laura chuckled, "I'll stick to Dan, whatever his name is; I can make believe I am in a Chinese restaurant."

They ate for a while in silence before Robert began to explain his plans for the rest of the week. He was required, at short notice, to attend a work conference in Birmingham, so tomorrow he would be catching a mid-morning train. He then went on to explain that although the conference finished on Thursday afternoon, he planned to stay an extra night, as there was a large record fair being held not far from where he was staying. So, that meant that he would be back late Friday, hopefully, he said, with a bag full of vinyl goodies.

Laura added, "I was planning to go and see my parents at the weekend, leaving here on Friday and staying over until Monday, so you'll have plenty of time to play the new additions to your library."

Laura was not asking for permission as that was the way they lived, happy for each other to have free rein to follow a life outside of their relationship.

"I'll miss out seeing your parents once again. Are you ever going to introduce me or are you that ashamed of me?"

"They can be difficult people," Laura answered. "They have some funny views, including people who live together should be married. We'd only get a lecture from them if we turned up hand in hand."

"I never realised they were puritans. So, they think I am just a friend, and we live apart?"

"It is more likely they don't ask questions and that way everyone is happy living in their own bubble. One day I am sure you'll meet them, but not in the near future. Anyway, why would you want to meet my parents, they're old people."

"I like old people," Robert commented, as he placed his knife and fork on his now empty plate.

"That's what I've heard as well."

Robert frowned, "Heard I like old people, from whom?"

"Sheila next door, your one-time lover, so I hear, she told me yesterday you and she had a thing going. I bet she really hates me for stepping in and spoiling things."

Robert laughed, "Dear sweet, mad Sheila. You do realise that she has, or should I say, she says that she has had affairs with at least seven of her neighbours in the street, as well as the man who comes around to sell her the Watchtower magazine, and the fellow who delivers her Tesco groceries once in a while. Oh, and not forgetting Peter, the tall good-looking man in the corner shop, the one who married the man of his life last year. I am just one of her odd fantasies that she likes to share. You've got to feel sorry for her, I know how hard it can be to look after someone twenty-four seven, it's not easy. So, far from hating you, I would imagine she likes you popping in and helping out."

"Ah, I thought I had found some dirt on you. I must admit I didn't really think she was your type. But you never really helped her out at all. I would have thought you would be just the right person to, you must have lots of sympathy having looked after your mother for all those years?"

Robert stood up, cleared the plates away, and walked into the kitchen as he spoke. Laura followed him.

"That was exactly the reason I found it so hard. I just did not want to spend more years being part of a caring regime for someone, I had had enough, and it is that simple really. That's why I volunteer at Age Concern a couple of times a month, I can feel I am helping, without getting too involved with people who need constant care."

Laura rinsed the plates and cutlery and placed them carefully into the dishwasher while Robert put the kettle on and prepared two cups. When they ate together, they would finish the meal with coffee and squares of dark chocolate. Laura stopped what she was doing, looked at Robert, and asked,

"Is that why you gutted this house after your mother died, you wanted to start afresh, clean the slate."

Robert leaned against the worktop thinking about the question. Even though they had lived together now for over a year, she had never really asked too much about his life and the decisions he had made before she moved in. He wondered why the sudden interest.

"Yes, I suppose it was a way of cleaning the house of all those dreadful memories. Bad memories that seemed to cling to the very fabric of it: my father hanging from the stair bannister, my mother trying to slash her wrists in the kitchen. Those images are still here for me, I guess they will fade over time, but they will never go away completely. So yes, ripping everything out of the house did help me to put some of those images to bed. But we are the sum of our past experiences, from that there is no escape, so we need to learn to live with those memories. Our recollections and our experiences make us who we are. That brings me on to my next announcement: I'm being me; I'm going to get a new car at the end of the month."

"Another one, yours is only, what, eighteen months old. You're not looking to change it already, are you? You must have money to burn."

"You know I always like to have the newest and the best, so it is the right time to jack in the old car and get a brand spanking new one."

"Tell you what you should do, buy some personal plates. With a name like Robert Carr there are lots of options. Then no one will know how old your car is. It could be ten years old, yet still look cool and ostentatious."

"RC ONE is not a good car registration number to get," Robert joked, then poured the hot water into their cups, while Laura grabbed a bar of dark chocolate, together they walked into the living room to catch the evening news on TV.

CHAPTER SIX WEDNESDAY

Thomas was now at his wits end. On Monday, he still had not heard a word from Laura. His fear led him to search through some of his old Filofax books, where he found the address for Laura Evans, or at least her address during the time they were dating. Thomas was not sure if he would find Laura still there. He recalled her parents and the problems that they encountered. Maybe they had moved to a place more suited to the disabilities that her father faced.

As the door opened, he was relieved to see that Mrs Evans was standing there just as she would have been when he was Laura's boyfriend. She squinted up at him. He explained who he was, or more precisely who he had been. She smiled as she then recalled the very nice man that Laura had once gone out with.

Thomas knew exactly what to expect as he walked into the Evans's household. He had visited four times before, when he had picked up Laura. Her grumpy father and her timid mother came as no surprise to him. What did astonish him was the revulsion her father now showed for his daughter. Thomas had only asked, what he thought was a simple question of her parents, where was Laura? At least when he had been her boyfriend, her father seemed to show a little pride in his 'little girl'. Today, Thomas was told abruptly by her father,

"I don't give a flying toss where she is. I want nothing further to do with the ungrateful little bitch." He turned back to the television screen, ending the conversation abruptly.

Laura's mother ushered Thomas away from the toxic tones into the kitchen apologising, as she always did, for her husband.

"He is getting a little worse now, I think it is the pain killers he has to take, but I do think deep down he misses Laura."

"You have no idea at all where she might be living at the present time?"

"Not really, she does send me the occasional letter, so I know she is well. When I write back, I have to send it to her godfather's address, she picks it up from him. The two of them were close when she was a little girl. I was surprised that she was using his address, as I thought my 'hubby' and he had fallen out many years ago. Mr Evans is a hard person to get on with. I can give you Tim's address if you like, or better still, I have the last letter that she sent me, that might help. I can give you that letter," she offered, while opening a kitchen drawer and dragging out an envelope from behind the utensils where it had been hidden. "I normally throw them away after a while, 'He' would not take kindly if he knew I was still in touch with Laura. Here, take this with you and maybe it will give you some clues. I have trouble reading her writing now, my eyesight you see, my next-door neighbour reads them to me."

Before he drove away, Thomas sat in his car and eagerly read the letter, hoping for any clue as to where Laura might be or what she was doing. It was a bombshell. He could not get the words out of his mind as he drove back to his shop. It explained a lot. She was leaving London, going away.

Dear Mum,

Well, things are starting to change very fast in my life once again. When opportunities appear, they should be grabbed with both hands, and that is exactly what I have done. To be honest, things are working out better than I could have imagined.

A deal has come up which will give me enough cash to leave London and set up home with 'Peanut'; our first opportunity to build a home of our own. I hope you are pleased and not too upset. I can now leave Robert, once and for all. I hope it does not hurt him too much, but I am sure he will find someone else who loves him. I'll be in touch, it might be a few weeks, but you'll hear from me.

Love, Laura xxx

The letter confirmed his worst fears. She had taken him for a ride, 'a deal has come up to give me enough cash to leave London'. Enough cash, he thought, one hundred thousand pounds of my money. He now urgently needed to find her, not for her safety, but for his. He needed that money back for his own wellbeing. Just who 'Peanut' was he had not a clue. As soon as he was back at the office, he was on the phone, talking once more to Mrs Evans. She could not help him at all, she had never heard of 'Peanut'.

Since Monday, he had called former work colleagues that both he and Laura worked with at the London Auction House. They could offer no explanation as to who 'Peanut' might be. In desperation, he contacted an insurance company that he thought she worked for occasionally, but they were unable to help him. He called Caroline, she too had worked at the London Auction House and was equally worried about Laura, but she could not add anything to help him identify just who 'Peanut' might be.

All he knew for certain was that he owed Howard Mullins one hundred thousand pounds. That money he had last seen with Laura. Now he could not locate her or the money. The time was fast approaching when Thomas was going to have to stand in front of Howard Mullins and explain exactly where the money had gone.

Once more he read the letter, earnestly looking for any clue that he might have missed. However hard he looked he could not see anything that might give the slightest hint to her mother, other than the name, who she was running away with. Thomas pondered. Was that a clue in itself? Did Mrs Evans know who 'Peanut' was, although she denied it? Thomas could not imagine the timid Mrs Evans could intentionally lie. 'Peanut' must be someone that Laura did not want her parents to know the identity of. A married man, that would make sense. Or even someone close to the family, someone, anyone, Thomas speculated, that Mr and Mrs Evans would not approve of.

His thoughts were interrupted by his phone ringing, he could see on his screen the name, Howard. This was the call he had been dreading and however much he wanted to, he knew he could not avoid answering it. It was Henry who spoke to him,

"Mr Mullins wants to see you about the matter of the loan he generously made to you last week. Be here tomorrow morning. Mr Mullins looks forward to receiving you, his money, and the payment of the agreed interest."

For Thomas, time was running out.

* * *

The difference between the way the Evans family lived their lives and Gerald Wallace lived his, was to Caroline's mind, criminal. It was as if they resided on two separate planets. However, disagreeable Mr Evans might be, no one could deny that he had almost given his life for his country. Fighting in the Northern Ireland 'Troubles' had left him having to rely totally on everyone around him. He seemed to have little help, little hope and little money. Here, in the expensive heart of London, Caroline followed Gerald Wallace through an opulent hallway into a large room, which he described as his drawing room. Everything had been accumulated by a criminal who was making a fortune by not playing by the rules. Was there any justice in this world she thought?

"So, young lady, what can I do for you?"

Referring to her as he had, 'young lady' indeed, did nothing to endear him to Caroline. She had been surprised when she had pressed the entry phone, with its camera pointing at her, that he did not ask what she wanted or who she was, his voice just emitted from the speaker, 'Please come up'. The door latch released with a loud buzzing and Caroline walked in. She hoped he was not expecting her.

"A friend of mine had a letter that was addressed to you in her handbag, and I was wondering just how it got there?"

"A letter you say. I have written many letters in my lifetime, as well as received a good deal more, could you be more specific?" He did nothing to hide the sarcasm in his voice.

"A letter telling you to buy shares?"

"Ah, your friend with the letter she stole. Is this the good cop/bad cop routine? Which one are you, you look bad to me, am I right?" He smiled, poured himself a whiskey and sat down in his favourite Chesterfield chair, leaving Caroline standing in front of him. "Greedy little cow, your friend, isn't she? Trying to jump on the gravy train after what she has done, is plain greedy, as well as naïve."

"What are you talking about, was she working with you, playing the stock market?"

"Why don't you ask her, so much easier, I'm sure."

Gerald sounded a little too confident, Caroline thought, she would remove some of that confidence.

"The contents are about insider share dealing, aren't they? Something you have plenty of experience at. Was Laura helping you out somehow?"

His look did not change, he seemed to Caroline to be a little too relaxed.

"Look, young lady, I'm not offering you a seat, a drink, or a warm welcome. You can bugger off now and tell your accomplice Laura, I am not succumbing to blackmail of any description."

"Blackmail, how was she going to blackmail you?"

"This is so tiresome, as well as pointless. Don't be so innocent young lady, I'm sure that both of you are in cahoots, you know what she knows and I know what I know. I think it would be wise for all of us to leave it at that and move on with our lives."

"I have no idea what you are talking about. I'm here to find out the whereabouts of my friend, Laura. The letter was found in her handbag, but sadly, she wasn't with it. I am thinking that you might have had an arrangement with her. I came here to see if you might know where she is."

"So, you're not some sort of tag team, bullying an old man, well that's a relief. But your friend was in the first instance trying to blackmail me. Then she tried again, as I am sure you know. If not, you'll have to ask her when you find her, unless she has done the dirty on you too. A word of free advice, she really is someone you should not trust."

He put his drink down, stood up and walked towards Caroline; she stepped back, uncertain of what he might do. He pulled a large cigar from his pocket and carefully lit it, blowing out a large cloud of blue smoke, before he continued.

"Looking at you, I sense you are not that close to her, or else you would know the whole story. The confusion in your eyes tells me you have no idea at all about what Laura was up to. So, let me tell you. You are very much mistaken about the relationship between myself and your missing friend. She was certainly not my partner in any criminal activity. This letter that seems to be handed around to everyone but the rightful owner, was the subject of a blackmail threat from your friend. I called her bluff. She went away. I have not heard from her since and do not want to hear from her again. Maybe the party who sent me the letter has taken things into their own hands, she was playing with fire, I can assure you. I have no idea and don't really care where she is. I presume you are leaving now."

Caroline had not considered that there might be another person. She had just assumed that the letter was typed out by Laura, and she was in the process of sending it to Gerald. The idea of a third person being the actual author had not occurred to her.

But why would Laura want to blackmail someone. In all the years she had known Laura, blackmail was not something she would have associated her with. The odd generous or conservative valuation to make a few pounds on the side of her auction house salary, well, that was one thing and useful pin-money. Blackmail was a whole new level.

Caroline turned and began to walk out, but then stopped at the door, turned back and looked at Gerald.

"How was she trying to blackmail you?"

"Best ask her when you see her. And when you do see her, tell her from me, if I go down, so will she."

"You're making no sense at all."

"Goodbye young lady, I've already told you once, ask your friend."

Caroline walked out of the door and into the street. She stood looking around the tree-lined street; it was clear he knew a lot. Her problem was he was not going to share any of what he knew with her.

* * *

Sheila sipped her gin and tonic with its ice and a slice, and the relaxation washed over her. It was three in the afternoon, her time. Upstairs her husband was sleeping soundly. She had pressed him long and hard in the early days to have an afternoon sleep, something he, at first, resisted. The technique of getting him into the bedroom, onto the bed, duvet over him, curtains drawn and lights out, every day for a week, had worked. From then on, just like a baby, he was ready for his afternoon nap. This gave Sheila at least an hour and a half to do whatever she wanted to without any interruption. A period to unwind, sip her alcoholic drink, although for the last few months it had become more than just the one. Well, she reasoned with herself, she deserved it, her husband was a burden to her.

Sheila often felt isolated. Her sister lived many miles away and rarely visited, never offered to help and still seemed just like the obnoxious younger sister she had always been. At first, some of the neighbours were kind, offering to help occasionally, but those offers had now dwindled away. In part she would attribute that decline to all the men finding her so attractive and flirting with her. She couldn't blame the men; she had always attracted looks of longing from the males she came into contact with. She refilled her glass. Yes, she recalled, Peter in the corner shop, she was sure he would have liked to continue their affair for longer. Still, it had been fun while it lasted.

It was Robert that she viewed as a permanent partner. She had been expecting him to make some sort of offer to her, even perhaps suggest a long-term relationship. Of course, the neighbours might think it odd, but Sheila had never bothered about neighbours gossiping. She would just tell them Robert was being just like a son to her, she would let their dirty minds do all the rest. The problem was Laura being around. Of course, she knew full well, that things would be so much easier if her husband was no longer around either. So, she made her mind up that things had to change, otherwise Robert and Laura might get too serious and become partners.

She had admitted to Laura about her relationship with Robert, she somehow hoped that such a confession would be enough for Laura to confront him, they would have a row about it, and she would pack her bags and go. When that did not work, thankfully, and sensibly, Sheila had a back-up plan. Last week she had started to put that plan into action. It had not gone fully as she had expected. However, the end result was exactly what she wanted. So now it was time to think about phase two.

She had read much about how to kill your husband and discounted all the bloody versions which included shootings and stabbings. There was also the poison course of action, which she did not think was appropriate for her husband, as she had read about some that cause pain, some that are so vile it is hard to get any spouse to swallow them and those which are slow working. The method she finally decided upon, was a simple pillow over the face, blocking the airways and causing death.

It would take, so she had read, about five minutes to be sure. Her husband would not have the physical strength to stop her. It would not cause him too much pain, maybe a little surprise, but he would soon lose consciousness. Tomorrow afternoon was going to be a good time, a little before the arrival of the doctor doing one of his regular visits to check up on her husband.

Sheila had played out the scenario in her mind many times. Her husband would be sleeping upstairs when she put the pillow over his face, denying him the air he needed to stay alive. The doctor would arrive an hour or so later, to discover her husband had died peacefully in his sleep. A fully expected death and no shock to the doctor, who would then write out a death certificate.

She would then be free to accept any proposal Robert might make, without the malicious gossip of the neighbours spoiling things. Thursday would be a turning point in her life.

* * *

Caroline stood outside the Banker Public House, took a deep breath and walked in. It was packed and noisy with lunchtime workers. Whenever possible, Caroline preferred to avoid entering any sort of public house alone or even in a group. She did not like pubs. This, she knew, surprised all her friends, they could not understand why she had such an aversion to them, especially as her parents had owned one and it was where she had spent her early childhood.

Maybe if her parents had shown a little more consideration towards her, they would not have allowed her into the bar whenever she wanted. As a young child, she recalled the attention she was given by the regulars, sitting on knees, being given sweets and fizzy drinks. Then when it was her birthday, she would end up with a table full of presents and cards, making all her friends jealous.

"Caroline, over here, we're in a quiet corner," she heard Andy shouting across the open crowded bar. His words sent a shiver down her spine.

"I'm glad you could make it. With all these work colleagues it's hard to get away from talking shop, I'm sure you'll give us something else to chat about." Andy then lowered his voice, "By the way, I have those things for you, stick around until everyone's gone and I'll go through them with you."

He led her through the throng, towards a large table beside a window giving a panoramic view of the Thames. Once there she was greeted by five men, all dressed casually, all a similar age – in their thirties, all reasonably attractive and all, but for one, were smiling at her. She thought they looked as if they were waiting to audition for a fashion magazine.

"Everyone, this is Caroline, my good friend and close neighbor." Andy rested his hand on her shoulder as he pointed to each of what he described as his team. "That's Harry, John, Peter,

Mike," each one acknowledged her and smiled, "and, of course, you know Robert."

She received only a cold acknowledgement from Robert.

Caroline sat down between John and Peter, who began to ask questions about her then, somehow, moving on to the subject of football, in which Caroline had very little interest. She looked across at Robert who was, deliberately, she thought, avoiding eye contact with her.

She began to recall the first time she had met Robert. He had become stuck in the lift with Laura, while it took two hours for the lift engineer to arrive and release the doors. All the while, Caroline, Andy and a couple of other residents were outside talking to the trapped occupants, trying to keep them calm and reassured. Once released, Laura and Robert, together with Caroline, had gone back to Andy's flat to recover from their ordeal. There, the four of them chatted through most of the night, with Laura questioning Robert about his life and his loves. It was clear that she had become very interested in Robert and that the two hours in the lift had given the two of them some sort of bonding.

Caroline remembered that Andy had introduced his friend that night as, 'Robert, who works in the same tall, grey building that I spend most of my day in.' Caroline had never really thought about it then or up until now. Robert was a part of Andy's team. They work together, in the same office, work colleagues. She had always assumed that they worked for the civil service in different departments, but she now knew they did not, they worked together. This changed everything.

"Sorry, we're boring you with our football talk," Peter interrupted her thoughts. "Do you work around here?"

"Up until a couple of weeks ago, just the other side of Cannon Street Station. I was a receptionist at the Royal Philatelic Society and before you ask, it was a job, I have no interest at all in collecting stamps."

"So, what's your plan?" Peter asked as he finished his beer.

"No plan really, just waiting to see where life takes me. I have a few ideas."

One by one, Andy's co-workers left to return to the office, until just the three of them were left. Andy walked towards the bar to buy another round, leaving Caroline and Robert together. It was Robert who spoke first. His voice hushed.

"So, now I understand where you were getting your information from. Andy has always been generous in using the company database. I should have guessed he helped you to find Laura's car."

"I never knew you worked directly together. If I had known, I would have thought you would have been searching through the ANPR cameras to see if you could find out what happened to Laura."

"That is firstly, illegal, and secondly, Laura left of her own free will, what gives me the right to stalk her and see where she is?"

"What's illegal?" Andy asked as he placed a beer in front of Robert, a lime and soda in front of Caroline and finally placed his own pint of ale in front of himself.

"You, doing favours for the general public," Robert pointed out, firmly.

"Come on, Rob, think of the good we can do by bending the rules a little. I would have thought you would have been the first to dig around to see where Laura has gone."

"What good would that do, all I would discover is that she is living with some fancy man, having the time of her life. What good would that do me or her, nothing at all. It was the end of the relationship and I'm now an ex-partner. I'm happy to leave it at that."

"So, what do you guys actually do in that office of yours?"

Robert spoke first, interrupting Andy as he was about to reply, "Nothing that you need to know about, or should know about."

"Come on, Rob, don't be such a stickler, we can tell her a little."

Robert stood up, leaving his drink untouched, told them both he was going back to the office, and that if he was ever going to lose his job, it was not going to be down to idle, loose gossip in a pub. They both watched him as he left.

"He's a funny guy," Caroline commented. She found him to be irritable, something that Laura had never mentioned before, but Caroline had noticed his moody behaviour over the last few days.

"He's a man in love, Caroline, that is the simple fact. I know he adored Laura and for her to up sticks and go off with some bloke, must be devastating for him. I kind of feel sorry for him, but he'll get over her, I'm sure. Anyway, you wanted some information about Howard Mullins and Thomas de la Mer, here's a copy of what I gave Laura."

"So, what do you do exactly, to be able to collate all this information?"

Andy sipped his ale as Caroline waited for an answer, she was not going to let this go easily.

"Rob was right, it is secret type stuff, not like MI5 or 007, but it is secret."

"And now the pub has quietened down, you and I sitting here over a quiet drink, friends and neighbours, you can't even hint at what you do." She waited, she knew Andy well enough, and as she expected, he caved in.

"Firstly, do not tell anyone," Caroline nodded. "Secondly, never, ever mention to Rob, 'Mister Goody Two Shoes' what I am about to tell you." Again, Caroline nodded in agreement as Andy resumed,

"OK. The government hands out big multimillion pound contracts to industry and companies across the country, that part is common knowledge. What the government try to avoid, not always successfully, is handing over a lucrative contract to a company only to discover there is some scandal arising out of it. Could be a director is a bigamist, the chief executive is on the fiddle; could be a cover for drug laundering. You can't imagine the things people get up to in business. So, our little unit checks on the companies and the management. We get told, say a month before a big contract is awarded, to make sure everything about the deal is kosher. So, we have to have access to an unbelievable amount of information and data, all at our fingertips."

"So, for example, you would know before anyone else, if a company is about to get a profitable government contract which, when it is announced, will see their share price rocket?" Caroline asked quietly.

"Well yes, that's true, but that is also very illegal. Alright, I help out a few friends: find ex-girlfriends, trace cheating husbands, making a few pounds on the side. But insider dealing is what you are talking about, that is in a different league altogether. If you're thinking of asking me to do that sort of thing, well, the rewards would need to be very high indeed for me to even consider it."

"Would Robert do it?"

"Robert, you're joking. He does not bend any rules, everything is done by the book with him. Why do you think Laura had to ask me about Howard, Gerald and Thomas? Robert was not going to help her."

"Did she say why she wanted to know about these three men?"

"Nope, just asked me to do her a favour, and it was a favour, no money was involved. By the way, I can look into her phone records if you like, they are always useful, if you think that might help."

Caroline picked up the buff file Andy had put on the table, folded it and squashed it into her handbag.

"I need to get going now. Yes, her phone records and anything else you think might be useful. I think she is in trouble. Those men she met last week, you've seen what they get up to, I am beginning to think she has fallen foul of one of them." Then, as she stood over Andy, she stopped and looked at him. "Can you do me another favour?"

"Yes, anything."

Caroline took from her handbag a scrap of paper, wrote down a name and date of birth, and handed it to Andy. "Can you find out as much about that person as possible?"

Andy looked at the name, "Sidney Stone, a relation?"

"My father."

WEDNESDAY ONE WEEK EARLIER

'A beautiful and recently updated two double bedroom duplex apartment set within a popular conversion of the old Royal Mail building. Being a conversion, this apartment boasts stunning original features such as exposed brickwork, pillars and beams. Situated on the banks of the River Irwell, the building is a short walk to Deansgate and the recently improved Victoria Station for rail and tram links across Manchester.'

Having read the estate agent's description, Laura thought Mirabel Street in Manchester was going to be her first choice, she was sure 'Peanut' would agree. She stuffed the leaflet into the glove compartment of her car, turned off the music and stepped out into bright sunshine cooled by a biting wind that swept Lennox Gardens. The Hurrell shares letter was her excuse to visit Gerald Wallace once more, but it was not the sole purpose of her visit.

This time with a large sum of money available to her, she was going to buy the statue from Gerald. She could not see him turning down the offer of a large sum of money for what he described as a bit of rubbish. Somehow, she would first need to get him to warm to her, their last meeting was strained to say the least. She hoped that by first offering him a deal around insider dealing she might get him on side. She would then step away from the letter and be able to focus on the statue.

She planned to start the offer at around thirty thousand then move up a bit at a time, with any luck she would have a fair amount of 'change' to give back to Thomas.

Just as before, Gerald let her in without question. It seemed that if a female was at his door knocking, they would be granted entrance, whatever their business. Given the last meeting she had had with him, he still appeared pleased to see her, leading her through the hallway into a small study, where he offered her a seat beside his wide, dark wood desk.

"So, come to apologise?" He sneered as he spoke, taking his time to look all over her.

"No, I have come to ask you once more, who sent you the letter, which I guess is telling you to buy shares in a company whose share price is about to go up?" She did not think for one moment that he was going to tell her. She had not planned for him to speak to her in any other room but the drawing room, where the figurine waited for her and she could casually bring the conversation around to purchasing it.

"I really cannot see what has changed since your last visit. Sorry, that is not true, I can see that your blouse is a lot more revealing than it was last week, trying the 'femme fatale' technique? Now, that might work."

"I draw the line at physical contact with dirty old men who can afford young tarts, so you're not going to get your grubby mittens on me." Laura told herself to be a little less confrontational, she was here for a reason, and the last thing she wanted was for an angry Gerald Wallace to throw her out before that figurine was safely in her handbag.

"So, if nothing has changed, you might as well leave now." Gerald stood, by way of encouraging her to go, but Laura remained firmly seated.

"Maybe something has changed. Maybe I know who sent you the information, maybe I am thinking that as it is likely to be a very profitable venture, well then, maybe I want to join the team, be part of your enterprise."

"There are a lot of maybes in that sentence, I can only add; why should I take a reduction in profit in order to take on a team member who contributes nothing to the team?"

"I'll add another maybe to the conversation; what if I said, maybe I can double your profits. Now would that thought encourage you to invite me to stay a little longer, maybe have a drink together and see if there is any way we can help each other."

Laura held back a smile as she watched his face change, she guessed he was thinking about the increase in profits. Gerald had two loves in his life, of that she was sure, profit and prostitutes. He invited her out of the confined study, along the hallway and into the drawing room, with its large bay window, sunlight filling the room. There was the sombre black ebony piano and not forgetting the four-thousand-year-old figurine, waiting to be plucked from obscurity.

She watched him pour her a large Irish whiskey, as she confirmed that the figurine was in the same place as it had been the last time she visited. It was still there, she rehearsed in her mind the conversation she was going to have with him. They again sat in the green Chesterfield chairs, he crossed his legs, had a mouthful of whiskey, and then asked her exactly what she had in mind.

"Well to use your analogy of teams, your team would remain the same. The difference would be I would also form a team, of which you and I would be the only members. The next time you get a letter from the anonymous sender instructing you to buy shares in a particular company, you, of course, do as instructed. Then, at the same time, you instruct me as to which shares to buy. I toddle off, purchase the quantity and then await the rise in share price. You profit from team A and Team B, simple really."

"How much do I get?"

Laura paused for a moment as if she was thinking, "Fifty fifty."

"The trouble with that plan," Gerald pointed out unhelpfully, "is that there is a danger that two buyers making a healthy profit on a regular basis, might alert those who oversee the stock market. You see we are not greedy people; Team A people purchase just enough shares to make a sensible profit, without flagging up anything untoward and so, effectively, we are keeping ourselves under the radar."

Laura, once again, had to stifle a laugh, 'not greedy people', she knew full well how greedy Gerald was, Andy Lane had given her a precise breakdown of the volume of shares Gerald had purchased and then sold in recent months. She could also clearly see, from the data that Andy had shared, that Gerald was pulling a fast one over his fellow insider dealer.

"So, let me get this clear, if you received the letter I have in my possession, you would buy thirty thousand shares in Hurrell Services, then split the profit with your friend when the price goes up, he or she no doubt, just to be sure, would ask for a copy of the transaction paperwork; well I would. Does he/she then know that you go off and buy, using another bank account, an additional thirty thousand Hurrell shares, making yourself a profit that is not shared with anyone?" Laura paused to see the effect her words were having before continuing, "I am sure the author of that letter would be very interested to hear just what you were doing, by your own admission, possibly flagging up to the authorities something suspicious."

A look of anger brushed across Gerald's face, his lips wrinkled as if he was sucking on a lemon, not drinking whiskey. Laura realised that she had become carried away with trying to outsmart him, in doing so she had put him into a sour mood.

"That is a very serious allegation you are making, linked, I would guess, to a threat."

What was she thinking? It was clear he was a greedy man, always wanting his own way, and showed very little respect to women. She thought again about the offer she had planned to make and realised that the moment she started to mention thousands of pounds, his eyes would light up. Her offer was a mistake; how could she try and be honest with a dishonest man; it was not going to work.

Could she just walk away without the statue? She should, that would be the right thing to do, give the money back to Thomas and continue saving for her new life with 'Peanut'.

She thought about the two-bedroomed duplex in Manchester. She wanted it for her and 'Peanut'. Thomas, who stupidly borrowed the money, would be out of pocket and want her to pay the interest on this failed deal, pushing the duplex even further away.

This was a moment; a moment in which she had to make a choice – she decided. She needed a diversion.

"Tell you what, Gerald, you go and get me some ice for this whiskey and while you're in the kitchen, have a think about the options: I join your team or I have a word with the author of that letter."

"You have no idea who wrote the letter."

"Come on, Gerald, how do you think I know so much about you? I do have other avenues to dig up information; you might recall a little earlier, I did say to you, 'maybe I know who sent you the letter.' Get me some ice and have a think."

His face still looking grim, Gerald stood up and left the room.

Laura had not planned any of this. She was not sure exactly how far away the kitchen might be, assuming that was where the ice was stored. Without any hesitation, she put down her drink, got to her feet and walked straight towards the decanter and the figurine that appeared to be relaxing on a pile of paper serviettes. She opened her large handbag, snatched up the reclining figure, quickly thrust it into the tissue paper she had already lined her handbag with, zipped it closed and turned to walk back to her chair. Then she heard the drawing room door start to open, she knew she would not make the chair without dashing across the room and drawing attention to herself. She turned towards the item nearest to her with a seat, the piano. She sat down quickly, lifted the cover to expose the black and white keys, and then played a scale on the keyboard, she continued to play a simple tune, 'Frere Jacques', as Gerald walked over towards her.

"Well you're no Liberace. Here's your ice," from his hand, he dropped two cubes into her drink.

Laura stopped playing and closed the keyboard cover before returning to her seat, her heart still pumping fast.

"Well," she asked, "what do you think?"

"I think you're a first-class bitch, who is intent on getting some money by whatever means possible. But however smart you might think you are; I really don't believe that you know who sends me useful information. After all, that is the only reason you came here in the first place. You are trying to trick me, and it is not going to work. In fact, can I say that you might well live to regret ever coming here in the first place."

"I'll take that as a no, then." She put her drink down, there was no way she was going to consume a drink in which there were ice cubes that had been in his hands, there was no telling what she might catch. "Ok, I'll leave you now and we'll see what the next few days bring."

"They could be a very difficult few days for you," Gerald continued to menace, "you are becoming a liability to me, have you ever consider how hard it is to walk with broken knees?"

Laura left the house with the valuable figurine in her possession, and the one hundred thousand pounds that Thomas had given her still intact. She knew together they would make enough money for her to ring the estate agent and put in a bid, but any elation was washed away by Gerald's threat: 'walk with broken knees'; that touched a raw nerve in her psyche.

She sat in her car sobbing loudly, her face buried in her tear-covered hands. She knew everything about walking without knees and legs. She had helped her mother care for her father over many years. Day in and day out, lifting him into a bath, washing him, drying him, feeding him, putting him to bed, doing almost everything for him, as well as sympathising and loving him. Both her and her mother were dedicated to him as a nun is dedicated to God. Yes, Laura had given the best years of her life to her father, sacrificed so much, only to be told when she wanted to start living her own life, begin to break free, that she was a 'selfish bitch, not fit to be his daughter'. In many ways, Robert could have been the perfect partner for her, both had given up their youth for a parent, both had trouble with relationships. They were similar in many ways, but that just wasn't enough for Laura. She was going to feel sorry for Robert when she left him alone, but she could see that their relationship could never be sustained, she wanted finally to live her own life in her own way.

She composed herself, wiped the smeared mascara from her eyes and drove across town to see Thomas, at least he had always understood her.

* * *

"Is that it?" Thomas asked as he held the small figurine in his hands, "and you expect to get three hundred thousand for this. Are you sure?"

"For someone who gets excited about dark wood furniture, with odd shapes carved into it, I don't think you are best placed to decide how valuable that beautiful statue is."

"But it looks modern, nothing like a four-thousand-year-old sculpture. If anything, it reminds me of a Henry Moore, and none of his sculptures are anything like a thousand years old, let alone four of them."

Laura laughed, took the Cycladic figure from Thomas, and placed it carefully on the desk in the cramped back office of his shop.

"Well, you do have a point, all Cycladic figures, from whichever island they come, have a modern look about them. Maybe the old adage, 'nothing is new' applies here."

"Well, full marks to you Laura, if this works out and you get your asking price. I, for one, would have stuck it in the window for fifty quid."

"And you would kick yourself when you found out exactly what it was worth. Tomorrow it will no longer be ours and we will be splitting a handsome profit."

Thomas pulled his phone from his pocket and pointed it at the figurine. "A keepsake," he explained, as the camera flashed.

"Did you really think I would double-cross you?" Laura asked as she gathered up her prize and returned it to the tissue in her handbag.

Thomas looked at her, he had to admit his feelings for her always ran deep, but however misguided his trust might be, the fact was, he did trust her. Of course, she was known to have carried out a few dark deals at the London Auction House, but he was not going to hold that against her. He doubted there was anyone in the world who was totally without a blemish on their soul.

"Large sums of money can be a temptation for anyone," he smiled, "it's just a shame I can't tempt you back to take up where we left off."

"You're a dreamer, Thomas, and one day that dreaming will get you into trouble. Goodbye."

Laura kissed him on the cheeks and left, leaving him alone in his shop. She was right, he thought, it was the dream of being with her that had encouraged him to acquire a hundred thousand pounds for her, without the slightest idea of just where she was going with it. In the same way, he had now watched her walk out of the shop with the very item he had helped her to buy. She would be back tomorrow with a large amount of cash, or would she? The niggling doubt that had been residing at the back of his mind for the last few days surfaced and pointed out, did he really know what it might be worth? He had no idea. Maybe it was time to Google Cycladic statuettes. His heart told him he was wasting his time, but the more rational part of him thought it prudent to check.

Wednesday night.

It was just before midnight when Caroline heard the doorbell ring. She had only just finished reading about the exploits of Howard Mullins and Thomas de la Mer; their crimes, their activities and Howard's clear lack of compassion for other human beings. The pursuit of money seemed to outweigh any common decency either might have once had. They were both criminals, shrewd criminals, who had so far managed to avoid conviction, save for the minor one they had each received which had given them a short spell in prison at the same establishment. Caroline now feared, more than she ever had, for Laura's safety. Laura had been dealing with people who had no moral code and who were, without doubt, dangerous. There was also a clear connection between Howard and Thomas. Caroline knew Laura was selling the statue to Howard, but she could not be sure of Thomas's part in the plan.

The doorbell rang once again, Caroline looked through the small spyhole in the door. To her relief she saw the distorted face of Andy.

"I'm sorry to call on you so late, but I saw your light was on and thought you would not mind if I popped in," Andy explained as he sat down.

"No problem, I have just been reading what people in the criminal world get up to."

"And can get away with," Andy added. "People who do not play by the rules and are clever enough to avoid detection. They are often well known to the authorities, but they don't have enough concrete evidence to convict them."

"Did Laura ever say why she wanted this information?"

"I told you, she never wanted to tell me. I did ask, well, she was a friend and I could see they were not nice people. Even so, she never told me what her business was with these men.

"I now have the information you asked for about Sidney Stone, your father."

Caroline looked at him, she could feel the rush of blood to her head, she was about to find out something she had lived in ignorance of since she was twelve years old.

She recalled that night as she had done on countless previous times, her father had tucked her up in bed, saying how he hoped that she was looking forward to the cinema at the weekend, then left her alone in her bedroom and returned to the public house downstairs which he ran with her mother. That had been the last time she had seen him.

The following morning, a young Caroline got up, dressed, and went downstairs to their kitchen to prepare her breakfast. She was confronted with the vision of her mother swaying, holding onto the sink, and crying loudly. She put her arms around her mother asking why she was so upset. She saw that her father was not sitting on his chair in his usual place at the table reading the morning paper.

With her daughter beside her, the older woman composed herself and explained that Father had left to join the army. He had left late last night and might be in touch when he got posted. All these years later, Caroline could still feel the confusion and dismay that she knew at that time. He had never mentioned the army, never hinted he wanted to leave the pub. Caroline had a tirade of questions for her mother, but each one was met with a thicker, taller wall of no explanation apart from the recurring answer: 'He has joined the army'.

Caroline could not focus clearly on her schoolwork, her friends, or anything else. The only thing she could think about was the question of just why her father had joined the army. Three days after her father left, things became much worse when her mother sat her down at the kitchen table and told her daughter that Father had been killed in action. She then added that as he died abroad, he was being buried there, which meant they would not be able to attend his funeral. Caroline watched her mother stand up and go about her cooking chores, as if informing her daughter that her father was dead was an everyday occurrence.

Every time Caroline asked a question, she was given the same stock answer: 'He was killed that is the end, grow up and get over it.' But Caroline could not, she could not comprehend what had caused her father to leave them. In the end she gave up trying to understand and accepted that her father was never coming back.

Her mother managed the pub on her own for two weeks before another man came into the household to help her run things, but it was not long before he became Caroline's stepfather as well. She got on well with him and none of them spoke of Sidney Stone ever again.

"Where was he killed?" was the first question she asked of Andy as he sat in front of her. His heavy-set jaw, full of dark stubble, dropped.

"Killed! Why do you think he was killed?"

"He joined the army and was killed in service, that's what my mother told me. I have tried before to trace him," Caroline attempted not to make it sound like an excuse. "Several years ago, I trawled through army records, but I found nothing. I even searched for him in the air force and navy. I guess I made up all sorts of different and complicated reasons as to why I could not trace his service record. Plus, I didn't want to ask my mother too many questions about him, she made it clear, she never wanted to talk about him."

"Well, in that case I need to tread a little carefully with what I have found out."

"What do you mean?"

"You just gave me a name and a date of birth, that was what I worked with, and I can tell you I couldn't find a Sidney Stone, with your father's birthday, in any of the armed services or emergency services."

"I don't understand, my mother told me he was killed in action; was he a spy or something?"

"OK, Caroline, sit quietly and I will tell you what I have found out about your father, and I am sure he is your father, as his national insurance number matches the one he had when he ran the pub. Sidney Stone, your father, is still alive." Andy stopped and waited.

"Alive?" Caroline could feel her pulse speed up.

Andy continued, "Your father was never in the armed services, he left the pub and started working as a night shelf-filler at a Tesco warehouse." Once again, he stopped and waited for Caroline.

Caroline took in this next snippet of information, "in London?" she asked in disbelief.

"West London, worked there for just under two years before moving on to working in a pub. In fact, over the next few years he was always in work doing some sort of bar work. He still is working part-time at a Wetherspoons pub just a few miles from here."

"Are you sure, Andy, my dad is alive."

"One hundred per cent, I am sure it is the same Sidney Stone you asked me about. There is not a lot more on him in the databanks. No criminal record, no parking tickets, oh, he does have a driving licence, clean as a whistle, plus, a good credit rating. Very much mister average, he has just led a straightforward, uneventful life and is far from being dead."

"Did he marry again?"

"Nothing on the books, but it's not uncommon to live with someone these days. There are two names on the electoral register at his address, I have it here; I imagine that you'll be planning to see him soon."

Andy gave her a sheet of paper with an address printed on it. "Not that far away, is it."

Caroline could not think of what sort of emotion she should be exhibiting, confusion consumed her. She had been expecting that Andy would just confirm that her father had died in action, many years ago. In fact, the very opposite was true.

"So why did he leave the family?"

"That question you'll have to ask him when you see him. Caroline, where do you keep your alcohol? You look as if you could do with a drink."

As he poured a small vodka and handed it to her, he said, "By the way, the password you gave me, the one that you said Robert tried on Laura's laptop, it didn't work on her mobile either, any ideas?"

* * *

'They say you'll never miss love 'till it's gone.'

Robert listened to the words of the song as he cradled a glass of red wine. The lyrics seemed to be very poignant. Was it only last week that he had talked to Laura about buying a house in Surrey? He had often dreamed of moving out of his parent's old house with its dark shadows, but while he was living on his own, it never seemed the right thing to do. Maybe part of him felt his parents, although dead, were still watching him and would not approve of him leaving the area, leaving their house behind. When Laura moved in, she brought a warm light to the house that invaded the shadows, no corner ever seemed gloomy again. The house was bright and relaxing, something it had never been all the time Robert lived there alone.

In his quiet moments, Robert had thought about the future with Laura, a larger house, maybe a small family, certainly two dogs, one a King Charles Spaniel, the other a black and white Border Collie. The garden would be large, divided in half, with the half furthest from the house turned into a vegetable plot. That was the ideal situation for Robert, family, dogs and your own produce. He would, of course, still work at his job, it was well paid and interesting with lots of benefits. Laura could follow her love of antiques, although she would not be able to go off too often with a family to look after.

That had still been his dream last week, he had even started to talk to Laura about it. She seemed keen, not over-excited, but certainly keen.

Now everything had changed, she was gone, never to return. All the time she had lived with him, she had been conspiring behind his back, planning and plotting, following her own agenda, which clearly did not include him.

Robert refilled his now empty glass and changed the record, he wanted something mellow. He chose the Hank Dogs, then settled back into his chair, alone, a place where he so often found himself.

After last Thursday, Robert was happy to let things be, accept what had happened and plan his life without Laura. Although now he found himself amongst people who wanted to find her and this stupid statue thing that she was buying or selling. Why had she even started doing such a thing? He could provide her with money, so for what possible reason could she have wanted to make such a large sum on the side. Her affair with some other man? Robert suspected that Thomas was not being as honest as he might be; he guessed that he would be Laura's type. He was just concerned what else Caroline would dig up as she ferreted around Laura's life. He feared that what she might find out about his lovely Laura could destroy his memories of her. As his third glass of wine started to take effect, Robert's mind ran through many possibilities and scenarios. She wasn't coming back, so why was everyone so interested in this statue? Maybe he should join the hunt.

CHAPTER SEVEN THURSDAY MORNING

Last night Robert had decided that he wanted to find out as much as he could about the Cycladic figure that Laura was selling to Howard Mullins. He had searched several academic websites, online museum resources and the major auctioneers. He learnt that there were many types and variations of these figurines. They all fluctuated in price dramatically, from just a few thousand pounds, to well over one million pounds. Robert regretted not asking more about the one that Laura was selling, all he knew was that she was getting three hundred thousand pounds for it. Was it worth just that?

If he had one question since Laura disappeared from his life, he now had many more. Not least why she had a letter to Gerald Wallace in her handbag giving him instructions to buy a number of particular shares in a certain company. Where did she find that? How had it fallen into her hands? What had she planned to do with it?

What about Caroline, a friend who is worried about an ex-flatmate, or so she says. What was her real interest? He guessed Caroline was not unintelligent, her experience at the London Auction House might well have given her an insight into the true value of the statue. Maybe they were selling it together. They would have stood to make a lot of money between them. He wondered if her interest lay more in finding that statue than in finding Laura. She had been playing Andy along, getting him to find things out for her, so a cunning woman for all the innocence she portrayed.

Then there was Thomas de la Mer, the ex-boyfriend that Laura had never mentioned, not once during their time together. When he and Caroline had visited his shop, he had acted innocent enough but had said very little in response to their questions. Nothing, Robert thought, appeared to be innocent where Thomas de la Mer was concerned, another ex-London Auction House worker. There Robert saw the connection, somewhere between the three of them, there was a statue worth a lot of money that Howard Mullins was still waiting to buy. Thomas and Caroline, no doubt, only wanted to find Laura in the hope of getting the statue back. So much for loyalty and comradeship.

Now in the cold light of the morning, following an agitated night of little sleep, Robert decided it was time he did something positive. Stir things up, shake a tree or two, bring this thing to a conclusion, so he could get on with his life. First, he called Andy, explaining that he was not feeling well and taking the day off. He then set about opening every drawer, every cupboard, every closet, digging around, sifting through clothes and boxes. He pulled everything out of the freezer. He carried on searching until he was certain that the much sought-after figure was not in his house.

There was one other possible place that the statue might be. He first looked up a timetable on the web, then went into the garage and recovered his fishing rods and all the associated paraphernalia that went with them.

It was while he was in the garage that his phone pinged; an email had arrived. He stopped arranging his fishing rods and looked at the message: it was from Andy.

'I know this will not meet with your approval, but I am just trying to help. The last message Laura sent from her mobile was about 8pm last Thursday; it read, *'Peanut', all sorted, Friday we will have all the cash. See you as planned Saturday L xx.'*

He had been right; Laura was planning to elope with someone else. Robert felt the anger growing inside him as he threw his fishing rods into the boot of his car. Today he was going to end this once and for all.

* * *

Thomas hoped he only appeared to be nervous, not terrified which was how he felt inside as he followed in the wake of Henry the Hulk through the hallway and into the kitchen where Howard Mullins was enjoying his morning coffee.

Thomas stepped into the kitchen, he looked to the left and was immediately dazzled by the white gloss surfaces of the modern kitchen units, the white tiles and the bi-fold doors that were fully open, allowing the fresh morning air and rays of sunshine to illuminate the large kitchen. He looked to the right and saw a long pine table, with six pine chairs, alongside a plain orange-painted wall, all such a contrast to the other side of the room. He was stunned by the size of the room which was bigger than his one-bedroomed flat.

At that moment he no longer felt like a successful drug dealer and criminal, that description was just his own illusion. He knew he would never be more than a puppet to those who manage and manipulate criminals. However much he might try to fool himself, the shop was owned by Howard, the drugs were supplied by a south London wholesale dealer and all Thomas did was sell and take all the risk. All for rewards that did not fit the risk he took or match the opulence that Howard and others lived in. The reality was Thomas was no more than a retail shop assistant, albeit selling illegal items.

"Come and join me." Howard waved Thomas to sit at the large pine table, where he sat pushing down a cafetiere of expensive smelling coffee.

As Howard pushed a white china cup and saucer of coffee across the table, Thomas thought he looked just like the rich fat-cat he was, smiling smugly.

"I expected you to walk in with a large rucksack full of cash for me, paying back your loan, with interest of course."

'Of course, you did,' Thomas thought, 'you are the sort of person who keeps one hundred thousand pounds in cash at your country retreat. I am just part of your cohort of money-making worker ants.'

"There has been an unexpected incident that is going to delay the repayment," Thomas admitted. He waited for the reaction; Howard's face showed no clues as to what he was thinking. Thomas continued, "I was hoping, given you have a lot of resources available to you, you might be able to help me out."

Howard looked up from stirring his coffee. "So, what unplanned circumstance has beset you?"

"The woman who was arranging the purchase of the item and the sale of it has disappeared with both my money..."

"Whose money?" Howard pointed out.

"Your money and the small figurine that was being sold. I have tried to locate her, without success. I was hoping that some of your people might be able to help locate her, the figurine, and your money."

"Thomas, let me get this right, you were in collusion with some woman, who you gave not an unsubstantial amount of money to, to go off and buy a figurine, you say, then she was going to sell it. I presume and hope you know where it was being acquired from and who it was being sold to?"

Thomas felt as if he was being questioned by a teacher. "No," he admitted.

"That is very remiss of you, Thomas. I would have thought that working for the London Auction House as you did, you would have been painfully aware that you should always know where an item was being acquired from and being sold to. First rule of illicit dealing."

"I trusted her." Then more meekly, "I thought she could be trusted. It's just that something has come to light that suggests she might have gone off with someone else, betrayed my trust. If we can find that person then maybe, we can get your money back."

Slowly Howard sipped his coffee, it was not hot, he liked his coffee to be milky and cool. He remained silent for almost a minute. Thomas was starting to fear that he was not going to get a good response from Howard.

"It is going to cost you at least five thousand pounds in extra interest if I am to help you locate her. Agreed?"

"Whatever it takes, there is a lot of mon... I mean your money, at stake here."

"What is this lady friend of yours selling? And what is her name? I need to start somewhere."

"Laura Evans, she was selling a Cycladic figure, a modern looking item, well I thought so, but it was four thousand years old, comes from some Greek island."

"I do know a little about such figures, plus I can tell you who she was selling it to."

"You know?" Thomas was surprised, he had hoped that the whole deal that Laura was arranging was going to be discreet; again, he was wrong about her.

"It was me. Just to be perfectly clear, we are talking about a certain Laura who you used to work with. She was selling a nice example of a Cycladic figure which I was looking forward to buying from her at a very reasonable price. The transaction was due to be completed last week, Friday, as I recall. She never turned up. I assumed that she had decided against selling that piece to me. I'm sure she had her reasons, some of which were touched on when she showed me the item in question. She was here last Thursday, I guess she never expected that I would have an expert here to examine the item, that did seem to alarm her a little. So, although we agreed the price, for your information three hundred thousand pounds, I suspected that she would not return."

"So, did you know where the item came from, first rule of illicit dealing?" Thomas said it before thinking, it sounded like a reprimand for Howard failing to follow his own rules.

Howard smiled, "Let's just say a pretty face tends to reflect brightly and blinds us men into not seeing the whole picture, or for that matter sticking to our own rules. I would guess she is the first woman you have watched walk out of your shop with a bagful of money, with no assurance that she is not going to rush along to some fashionable clothes shop and blow the whole lot. We all experience our gullibility sometime in our lives."

"So, was it a fake?" Thomas was a little relieved to hear that Laura was missing. If she was trying to sell a fake to Howard Mullins, then the consequences could have been even more catastrophic for him, for his part in the deal.

"In fact, it is the exact opposite, my expert suggested that it could well be a Schuster Master, a sought-after piece worth about one million pounds."

Thomas listened; his worst fear was coming to fruition; the statue had been worth a million pounds. She was duping him, leading him along. Why had he trusted her? He was a fool.

"Thomas, for the next part of this puzzle, who do you think she has run off with?"

Thomas took the letter that Mrs Evans had given him from his pocket and placed it on the table. Howard opened out the folded letter then began to read. When he finished reading, Howard carefully re-folded the letter and handed it back to Thomas. He re-filled his cup with coffee, adding a substantial amount of milk to it.

"Well I see the problem now. You say you have no idea who 'Peanut' is?"

"I have tried as best I can, no luck at all."

"Can I say, this is not an impossible problem to solve, just an irritation. It's just that an extra five thousand pounds will not cover the cost of my help. We'll discuss my full renumeration for helping you once we have the figurine back."

"Do I have a choice?" Thomas sounded resigned to the fact that he would never be more than a lowly operator in the underworld he resided in. Howard shook his head negatively.

"I am glad we are both agreed on the terms. I will get my man to visit 'Peanut' and see what they have to say for themselves."

"You know who 'Peanut' is?" Thomas was astounded to hear that Howard knew the identity of 'Peanut'.

"Henry," A smiling Howard directed his raised voice towards the hallway, Henry was never that far away from his master. "Come here, I have a job for you."

* * *

Even the hot water that cascaded over Caroline could not wash away the fatigue that hung heavy on her body. It had now been a whole week since she had heard from Laura, this was worry enough, then, last night, she learnt for the first time the precise nature of the people that Laura had been dealing with. It was no wonder Laura sensibly made a point of telling Caroline where she was going last week. Although, she had not given Caroline the finer details as to the type of business associates she was planning to work with. The more Caroline learnt about them, the more she feared for Laura's safety. Caroline had not slept well all week, last night, sleep had eluded her once more.

One person was again missing from her life when this morning another might be coming back into it. The first thing she planned to do today was to visit the address Andy had given her and see if his information really did lead to her 'dead' father, or just a cul-de-sac of hope.

All night she had thought about what she might say. What do you say to someone you thought had died years ago? It would not be an everyday conversation. 'Hi Dad, it's your daughter, grown up a bit, haven't I?' Too sarcastic. 'Why did Mum tell me you had died?" Too Blunt. Maybe a simple hug and a tear would speak volumes.

There was also that nagging doubt in her mind that the Sidney Stone she was going to visit, was not the same Sidney Stone that read her bedtime stories or let her dance on the bar. He could turn out to be a total stranger, bemused by a woman turning up at his door asking about her father.

She stepped out of the shower and looked at herself in the mirror, wet hair dangling down over her face. Would he recognise her? She was just twelve when he had leaned over her bed and kissed her goodnight, the smell of his aftershave hanging over her pillow. She was no longer that little girl; she was now a woman, a slightly overweight woman she believed, but nevertheless a woman.

With the nervous energy of a person getting ready for a job interview, Caroline dressed, missed out on breakfast as she just could not face eating, then picked up the tube to take her just three stations. He lived so near, maybe she had passed him while shopping at Tesco, even sat opposite him on the tube train. Or maybe in a city of several million people those sorts of things do not happen. Andy had told her that Sidney worked at a Weatherspoon pub, only part-time, doing some afternoons and late nights. As Caroline walked up to the address, she desperately hoped there would be a reply, and Sidney was not out shopping.

Clutching the only faded colour photograph she had of her father, she stood in front of the white PVC door. The house was one of a long row of terraced houses. The street was presentable, with the obligatory black rubbish bins alongside each door. The road was lined with cars, each with their residents parking permit firmly displayed. She wondered if one of the cars belonged to her father. With her pulse racing, adrenaline flooding her senses, she rang the doorbell. It seemed to be an eternity before the door finally opened.

The man stood looking at the woman in front of him, his familiar grey-green eyes examining her features. Caroline could see the same shaped face, the square jaw, the smallest of gaps between his two front teeth. He was older, well she was as well.

"Dad?"

"Caroline? My god, Caroline, my little girl."

She threw herself into his arms and held on as tightly as she could.

She sat opposite her father at the kitchen table as he served her a mug of tea. All she could do was look at him and wipe the constant tears from her eyes. He had seemed smaller than she remembered when she had hugged him at the door, she knew she had grown, and so he was no longer the tall man she once perceived him to be

"I think I should know how you take your tea, but you'll understand why I need to ask. The last time I gave you a drink it was more than likely some sort of squash."

"Milk, no sugar, as I have given up sugary drinks."

"So, this is a big surprise, I imagined that you wanted nothing to do with me."

"I thought you were dead. You were never far from my thoughts during all these years."

"Dead, is that what your mother told you?"

"Yes, killed when you joined the army."

"I shouldn't laugh but I could never imagine your mother looking at me and thinking soldier material, yet I suppose it stopped you asking too many questions. So how did you find out that I was resurrected?"

"I wanted to find out when and where you were killed, and how. I now know why I couldn't find anything online about you in the army. A friend of mine did some serious digging and, well, here I am."

"Well, I'm glad you're here now. I've always thought about you growing up and wondered what you were doing."

During the next thirty minutes or so, there were tears, there were awkward silences, over-enthusiastic words spoken and more cups of tea, as they tried to catch up on all those missing years. For now, they had to settle for just overviews and headlines.

Then as emotions settled, the first of the difficult questions was asked by her father.

"Well, I'd best be polite; how is your mother?"

Caroline answered, "She's well. They left the pub a few years ago, the trade tailed off." Then she asked her own awkward question, the question that had been on her mind all night. "Why did Mother tell me you joined the army and then were killed in action, when it seems you both just parted."

Sidney leaned back in his chair, not speaking for the moment. Caroline could see that he had put on a few pounds since her souvenir photograph had been taken, yet he still was an attractive man, just a few lines across his face and his hair only showing the first signs of grey.

"Maybe she was just looking for an excuse as to why I left, anything but the truth, for her that was the worst outcome. Had I known what she had told you, I might have been persuaded to come back and put the record straight. I can't imagine how you, as a young girl, coped with being told that I had died in action in the army. I guess the truth would have been better, but your mother had a very different view on the world to me."

"So why did you leave?"

He hesitated, once more, before saying, "I found someone else that I loved more than your mother, these things happen. I had married your mother when I was relatively young, you soon came along and then we started managing the pub. Everything seemed to be racing along at an incredible pace. The lives we live change us in ways we do not always see until it's too late. I realised that I could not spend the rest of my life with your mother. I carefully explained to her the whole situation."

"She could have told me you left her for someone else, it's not an uncommon occurrence. I think about three or four kids in my class at school had their parents' divorce."

"Oh, if it was that simple. Your mother wanted nothing to do with me and didn't want you to have any contact with me either. She took it all very badly, and I can understand why, but she was a little, how shall I put it, Victorian in her views. Caroline, you are not, you have youth and I hope tolerance on your side. I fell in love with a man and that's the truth of it. That was something she could never comprehend or accept. I was disowned, in a funny sort of way, from you all, never to be spoken of, as if I was some evil monster. Maybe if I had met him a little later in my life, when you were older, I could have explained it to you, but Mother did not want me tainting her little girl."

"You're gay?"

"Yep, my partner, Luke, is out at work. I work part-time at a pub and do most of the household chores. I'm a bit like a wife," he smiled. Caroline recalled the infectious smile she had seen so often on her father's face; it was reassuring to see that he had not lost it.

She threw herself at her father, hugging him as she felt the tears welling up in her eyes. Her voice was muffled as she spoke into his shoulder, "I'm so sorry I didn't push Mother harder for answers to the questions I had. If only I'd been more persistent then she might have told me. I thought she was dealing with your death and I just didn't want to ask too many questions for fear of upsetting her. I still love you and I am so glad I have found you."

"You have nothing to blame yourself for Caroline. It was your parents, both of us, our fault that we did not explain to you what was happening."

Father and Daughter laughed tears of joy, tears of relief, tears of welcome, until Caroline's phone interrupted their reunion. It was Andy.

"I'm sorry to trouble you, but Robert has called in sick today, which is so unlike him, I am having to cover a couple of his long-planned meetings. Caroline, I am worried, I just can't get away. Could you possibly pop around and make sure he's OK? I'm sure he wouldn't do anything stupid, but with Laura walking out on him, there's no telling. Plus, it looks as though she was having an affair. I managed to get into part of her phone account. I am really worried about his state of mind."

"Do you know who it is?"

"Not yet. So far, I have been only able to access her phone account and at first glance she was conversing with someone about going away. I need to cross check a couple of telephone numbers. As soon as I know more, I'll let you know. Will you go and see Robert for me, please, check-up on him, make sure he is OK?"

Andy, she thought, why ask me now of all days, when I am sitting alongside the father, I thought had died years ago. Can't it wait. Can't I ignore helping someone, who has been less than enthusiastic about finding Laura, someone who has needed to be pushed to get involved all the time. But she knew she could not refuse a humanitarian request, that was her all over. So, reluctantly, she agreed, looked at her father, and hugged him tightly again.

"I've got to go, there is something I have to do to help someone. But now that I know where you are, you're going to see a lot more of me, I promise. I have a lot to tell you as well."

Half-heartedly she left her father, to go back home to collect her car. Then off to see if Robert was alright. She fully understood what Andy was getting at. She knew what his real concern was. Roberts's father committed suicide, and maybe the son was just as susceptible.

THURSDAY ONE WEEK EARLIER

Understanding antiquities is complicated, Thomas knew that for a fact, which was why he focussed so much of his knowledge and time on the furniture of Thomas Chippendale. That way he could always be sure exactly what he was buying and what he was selling. Not that he needed to make a profit from his shop, there were other more reliable ways to make money; including having an ex-girlfriend involve you in a transaction selling an item which you might know little about.

A little figurine selling for three hundred thousand pounds, Thomas was impressed and interested. He Googled Cycladic figures, just to see what they were like and the sort of money they might fetch, knowing that Laura had told him she was selling a little under what the market might pay, in order to ensure a quick sale.

He learnt a little more about the figurine, which added to what Laura had already told him. The Ashmolean website talked about their example of a Spedos type figurine that had faint remains of painted eyebrows and hair. It also confirmed his own suspicion that the style of these artefacts inspired people like Modigliani, Giacometti and Hepworth as well as being collected by Moore and Picasso. He recalled Laura words: 'nothing is new'.

He then tried to find one for sale. There were not any he could find currently, but he found one a similar size to the one he had handled which made only sixty-two thousand at auction. The next one he looked at; he almost fell off his chair in shock. It was bigger, and in better shape than the first one he had seen, it appeared to be in the same sort of condition as Laura's figurine exhibited and it had sold for one point two million pounds.

Thomas displayed both the million plus figure with the picture of the one that Laura was selling on his computer screen. To his untrained eye they looked to be the same, but for the relative size. Was size that important with these things? He had no idea. If Chippendale had made one of these figures, he would have known, at once, the value.

His lack of knowledge frustrated him. He had trusted Laura to make all the judgements, decide the value and carry out the sale, as well as purchasing it in the first place. Had his trust been misplaced? Would Laura rip him off? He only had her word regarding the selling price. More than a million pounds was a long way from his share of one hundred thousand pounds.

Thomas thought long and hard, he did trust her, why shouldn't he? She had always been honest with him in the past, she even had a pet name for him. He still had feelings for her, he knew how hard her life had been with her tyrannical father and nervous mother. Thomas often wondered if it had not been for her parent's problems, would she have continued their relationship. It was a question he might now never get answered.

He pushed aside his romantic aspirations for her and thought about the cold fact that a lot of money was at stake. Money in large amounts can change people; it warps their morals. Maybe the temptation of a very large profit had tempted Laura to be less than frank with him over the price she was getting. Thomas needed to speak to someone who might know a little more about Cycladic figures, the only person he could come up with was Howard Mullins. Howard had a wide knowledge as well as many years' experience. Thomas picked up his mobile, only to be interrupted by the light sound of the shop bell, a customer had entered.

Gerald Wallace stepped into the shop, looked around and was relieved to find there were no other customers present. Other people casually browsing made him nervous; he could never be entirely sure who they might be. The last thing he wanted was for some undercover police officer to observe him obtaining his special therapies.

"Gerald, what can I do for you?" Thomas asked, putting his phone down and walking across towards his customer.

"Morning, old boy, thought I'd pop in and pick up a few bits for the weekend. Got a very special party planned," Gerald smiled. It had been a stressful week for him so far. He recalled the good-looking woman coming around not once but twice, trying to muscle in on the lucrative little arrangement he had going. He had soon seen her off. Yet it did worry him a little that she was aware of what was going on.

He remembered the telephone call he got out of the blue, someone offering an arrangement in which both of them could profit. At first, Gerald thought it was some sort of scam. But when the person on the other end of the phone gave a very detailed breakdown of Gerald's chequered past, he had listened carefully.

"What have you got planned, your usual weekend of debauchery?" Thomas asked.

"Hired a couple of very attractive Chinese girls for the weekend, so I will need a little something to make the party go with a zing."

"Not a cheap weekend then?" Thomas pointed out.

Gerald was fully aware, as was Thomas, that all his indulgences did not come either cheap or legal; he had no worries on either side of the fence. He had the money, that had never been difficult for him, his family was rich to start with. He had continued pulling in profit however he could, breaking the rules had never been an impediment for him. In his younger years his wife had been the biggest drawback to him enjoying life. He had never really wanted to marry and had done so only because that was what was expected of him.

Once his father died, he quickly divorced his wife and got on with life. It was her he suspected of alerting the authorities of his special share dealing techniques and got him banned from the city. That was one of the reasons he now avoided any sort of relationship. If he wanted sex, he paid for it, which was a lot less hassle than getting into a relationship. Plus, if he really wanted to, he could hire two or three women at a time. His ex-wife would never have agreed to that.

"Well, I guess you'll want some extra stuff today then?" Thomas enquired.

"I'll have full oz of coke, that should see me through."

"Sounds like you are trying to impress as well. One day Gerald, you'll kill yourself surrounding yourself with young girls."

"We'll just pray that day is a long way off, or you'll lose a good customer," Gerald was so relaxed he patted Thomas on the shoulder and noticed his own unusual smile reflected in the mirror of a mahogany dressing table. He still thought of himself as an attractive man, it did not matter what the girls he employed thought.

"Come into the back office and I'll get you prepared for the weekend ahead."

Gerald followed his high-class dealer into the back office and stood beside the desk as Thomas knelt beside a cabinet, opened the door and pulled out a small box. Gerald glanced around the room, nothing much had changed since the last time he was here; it always looked the same: cluttered. He then looked at the computer screen, taking a fleeting glance at the image displayed.

"You look at some really weird porn, old boy."

"Not porn," Thomas sounded a little muffled from his position on the floor, facing the ornate cupboard with its wooden inlay, "a bit of research."

Gerald peered at the screen; the image looked familiar; he just could not place it. "What is it, a modern sculpture? I thought you were into old wooden chests."

Thomas stood up, clutching a small plastic bag. "It looks modern but in fact it is bloody old, four thousand years old, from the Greek islands, this one might be from Naxos."

Gerald examined the image even closer. "My father spent a lot of his youth there, God knows why. Where is it now, in a museum?"

"No, it's part of a deal I'm involved with."

"What, you're selling it?"

"Yes, for a healthy profit as well. This shop doesn't come cheap, so any profit is handy."

"Where did it come from?"

"Don't tell me you fancy buying it. Us dealers don't talk about where our items originate from."

Gerald finally recalled where he had seen it before, he wanted to shout, but decided to remain calm for the moment. He moved his face closer to the screen, squinting slightly as he examined the displayed image.

"Tell me Thomas, what are the chances of having two of these old things having exactly the same marks, flecks of paint, chips and cracks?"

Thomas stood beside his customer before replying, "I would guess almost impossible, if it's an original. Think of all my furniture, handed down through generations, each chair or table living in different households. Different scratches and marks all add to their value, making them unique."

"Where did you get it?"

"Told you, I protect my sources."

"Not if it's been stolen, you don't. That is mine, I have had it sitting next to the decanter for the last decade or so, my old man left it to me with a load of other, what I thought was, rubbish. I am certain it's mine, down to the missing feet."

"Are you sure, Gerald?"

"Of course, I'm bloody sure. Where did you get it? And don't give me any of that dealer crap, where did you get it?"

"A friend of mine, she purchased it all legitimately, I gave her the money for it."

Gerald began to recall the last time he had seen it, certainly last weekend, of that he was sure. He had spilt some soda water and lifted it up to take some napkins to mop up the spill. A woman, he thought, Harriet his cleaner had been with him for years, so he discounted her for the moment.

"Does your friend have brown hair, shoulder length, a good body with slender legs and a seductive perfume?"

"Maybe," Thomas sounded nervous. He picked up his phone, flicked through some photographs and showed Gerald a picture of Laura.

"That's the bitch who visited me, twice, and nicked it, stole my whatever it is. Where is it Thomas? I want it back."

If Gerald was going to be honest with himself, he had never been bothered about what he considered to be a bit of rubbish, just another one of the many items his father brought back from overseas and cluttered the rooms of his childhood home with. However, he knew that if Thomas was taking an interest in it then there was money to be made, and Gerald had never been the sort of person to avoid making money.

"Are you sure?" Thomas asked as he looked again at the computer screen.

Gerald assured Thomas, in strong terms, that he was certain that it was his statue on the screen. He then pointed out, to dispel any thoughts that Thomas might be harbouring that this Laura person was acting honestly, that she knew a lot about his background and current predilection for recreational drugs and had threatened to use the information against him. He also pointed out to Thomas that she, no doubt, had some idea where he bought his drugs from.

"She did mention my second income here, as well as other stuff. I just thought she was interested in me," Thomas admitted, as much to himself as he did to Gerald.

"Listen to yourself, you sound like a lovesick schoolboy. How much of your money did she supposedly spend to buy this piece?"

Gerald was surprised to learn that Laura was supposedly purchasing the statue for one hundred thousand pounds. As if that was not enough, Thomas disclosing that she was selling it for three times that amount, pushed Gerald into a full rage, his face reddening.

"Where do I find this bitch?"

"Hold on Gerald, don't forget she has one hundred 'grand' of my money."

"I don't give a shit about your money; she has screwed both of us. Where do I find her?"

Thomas acknowledged that he did not know exactly where she was at the present time, or even where she lived. He told Gerald that she should be calling in this afternoon with the proceeds of the sale and suggested he could hang around and wait for her.

"You might want to hang around like a puppy dog waiting for her, but I doubt you are going to see any of the money that she is getting for the statue. She needs a lesson taught to her; she thinks she is so clever; I'll change that. I have a friend who can find people with some sort of phone technology or something, he'll tell me where she is, and I'll have it out with her, wherever she might be." Gerald seized his small bag of drugs from Thomas, "This, I'm taking as a gesture of goodwill."

"I'm sure she'll be here later," Thomas did not sound convinced.

Gerald ignored him and stormed out of the shop, slamming the door behind him. When he found this Laura person, she was going to get a damn good slapping.

*　*　*

"Who's he?" Laura asked.

Howard turned to look behind him, he had to twist slightly awkwardly and look up at the man standing at the back of him. Howard

118

had chosen to receive Laura in what he described to everyone as his day room, in fact, it was more commonly referred to as a reception room. It was the larger of the two reception rooms located on the ground floor. Howard's day room was a rectangle spanning one side of the house. The front bay window overlooked his gravel drive and the double glass door at the other end overlooked the garden. In between them was a fireplace, flanked by two large beige-coloured sofas. Howard sat in one, with his other guest standing at the rear of him, like some large ornament.

"Him?" Howard turned back to look at Laura. He might have always had bad eyesight, but he had always been able to appreciate a pretty girl like Laura. "He is my expert I told I was getting. You can't expect me to buy something for a lot of money without having its authenticity confirmed. That would be plain silly and foolish. Please, take a seat."

He watched Laura as she sat opposite him on the matching sofa. Today, he was not going to offer her a drink of any sort, he wanted her to feel nervous and uncomfortable, which was how she seemed to be already, very unlike the confident person who, just last Saturday, was bouncing up and down on his bed, although not in the way Howard would have liked her to. Maybe the statue was a fake after all.

"So, where is this four thousand-year-old item of interest?"

Laura opened her large handbag and fumbled with some tissue before finally taking out the buff-coloured ornament with its feet missing. She leaned forward and handed it to Howard. He looked over the item, viewing it from every angle. He examined closely the pale traces of paint on the face and looked carefully at the legs without feet. He liked what he saw, it looked to be the real thing, a small figure from one of the Cycladic islands. Casually he passed it over his shoulder to the short, stout, bespectacled man behind him.

"What do you think?" Howard asked.

The bespectacled man moved towards the bay window, intently examining it under the bright sunlight.

Howard looked at Laura, "One question I would like answered. The origin of that marble lady, from where does she come?"

"The Cycladic Islands, possibly Naxos."

"Mockery does not become you Laura, you know full well what I mean. From where did you get the piece? Who owns it? Why are they selling it? It all helps me build a picture."

Laura shuffled on her seat. Howard could see that she really was nervous, he wondered why.

"I told you before, I'm selling at a discount price to you and only you. The understanding is that you pay me in cash and don't ask those sorts of questions. You just have to trust me."

"Come now, you know me, who I am and what I do. I always ask where an item has come from and in turn want to know who it is being sold to. That is the foundation of what I do to ensure I am not getting caught out. I am planning to buy it; I just want to know who is selling it?"

"They do not want to be identified."

"Although I am getting a good discount for going without that information, part of me is saying that I should pay the full price and get to know the seller."

"Do you want it, or not? Make your mind up."

"Don't be impatient, my man by the window needs to finish his assessment first. We'll just have to wait; you cannot rush true experts."

They sat looking at each other in silence for a few minutes, as they waited for a verdict from the bespectacled man, who had now taken his herringbone jacket off, and was consulting a small laptop.

"My invitation for a weekend away in Birchington still stands, a quiet, restful weekend of good food and good music," Howard smiled as he broke the silence between them.

"I am not sure I would consider Wagner as good music; I'll take a rain check on your offer."

"Ah, a rain check, another one of those irritating American phrases that has invaded our language. Did you know that the expression 'rain check' originated in the 1880s? If it rained heavily enough for a baseball match to be postponed, the ticket holders were given a 'rain *check', a coupon to attend the next match. So maybe when it is sunnier, you'll take up my offer."*

Howard could see that his trivia facts only served to irritate Laura.

The bespectacled man, now in his shirt sleeves, positioned himself in front of the fireplace. He cleared his throat; his small audience awaited his verdict.

"I have examined the statue in as much detail as I can, given the circumstances in which this preliminary examination is taking place."

Howard, still smiling, turned to Laura, *"Fortunately, I am not paying him by the word."*

Bespectacled man adjusted his thin-framed glasses and continued, *"I am confident that this small figure is in fact a Cycladic marble female figure, dating from around two thousand years B.C. Carbon dating would confirm this further, yet it bears all the correct indications of its age through a visual inspection. As you might already be aware, this is the best-known type of Cycladic artwork that has survived the centuries. The marble figurines are of, most commonly, a single full-length female figure with arms folded across the front. The type is known to archaeologists as a 'folded-arm figure'. Apart from a sharply defined nose, the faces are a smooth blank. Although there is evidence on some that they were originally painted, as this example shows. Considerable numbers of these are known, though unfortunately, most were removed illicitly from their archaeological setting, which seems usually to be a burial place."*

As he spoke, he pointed out the details to his audience, as if they were students at one of his lectures. Then he continued:

"This particular example, Spedos type, so named after an early Cycladic cemetery on Naxos, is the most common of Cycladic figurine types. It has the widest distribution within the Cyclades, as well as elsewhere, and the greatest longevity. The values do vary greatly.

"Sculptors living on different islands produced marble figurines in a similar style but with distinctive variations. The recognition of different artistic personalities in Cycladic sculpture is based upon

recurring systems of proportion and details of execution. The figure we have here today, I believe, can be attributed to the Schuster Master, who was active sometime in the period around 2400 B.C. Over a dozen figures have been assigned to him. All of the figures display a head with a broad curving top and a crescent-shaped ridge at the back, a long aquiline nose, and well-defined knees," he pointed to each of the elements as he spoke. "The Schuster Master also preferred to show his figures with a slightly swollen belly, probably indicating pregnancy. Like all artists at this early period, the Schuster Master's real name is unknown, he is identified only by the style of his work. The sculptor takes his name from a figure once in the Schuster collection, the only surviving unbroken figure by this artist."

"All very interesting, but what is its worth, that is what I really need you to tell me." Howard was getting impatient, he had employed this expert to tell him if the item was genuine or not and what it might fetch at an auction, he did not want a comprehensive history lecture.

"As I mentioned, I believe it is a Schuster Master, although I would need to confer with my associates to input their valued opinion. If I am correct it is worth, given that the feet are missing, a little over one million pounds. I do add the proviso: subject to further discussion."

Howard turned towards Laura, "Interesting, does this mean you are going to put up your price or am I entitled to a very large discount? Oh, and David, thank you for your time, you can go back to your day job now. I look forward to seeing you again tomorrow."

David collected his jacket and laptop and left Howard alone with Laura, both of whom looked very serious.

"He has his opinion and I have mine. I gave you a price," Laura spoke seriously, "I'm happy to stick with that price. Unless you want to pay what your, so-called, expert valued it at?"

Why would she, Howard wondered, she had just been told by, in his estimation, a very well-informed professional that the item she was selling was worth over three times what she was asking for. They had known each other a long time, Howard was sure she knew that he was not short of a penny or two. Yet she did not argue or try to contradict the expert and still appeared happy to stay with the original asking price.

That made no sense to him and he guessed that would make no sense to anyone else, only to Laura, it would appear, did it make any logic.

"I have to ask myself two questions: firstly, why are you selling me a genuine Cycladic figure for well under its possible market value? Secondly, why are you so reluctant to tell me who is selling the item? I am really searching for an answer, Laura. Are you going to help me at all?"

"Do we have a deal or not?"

Howard leaned back into the sofa, his arm stretched out along the back of it, his fingers tapping the material. He only trusted one person in this world: himself. He looked at her eyes, searching for a clue, he could see no sign, she would make a good poker player, he thought.

"The thing is, what if, this is just a hypothesis, you give me a real bargain, then once it is safely sitting in my trophy cabinet, I get a visit from the police saying it is stolen. I get arrested and spend some time at her majesty's pleasure. What do you think?"

"I think, why would I do that in the first place?"

"Revenge."

"Do I strike you as a vengeful person?"

"Well, I wouldn't blame you."

For the first time Laura smiled. She placed the figurine on the octagonal coffee table in front of her and then leaned back, reflecting the same posture of relaxation that Howard was displaying.

"I suppose," she began, "you are referring to a certain incident that resulted in my being sacked from the London Auction House."

Howard nodded in agreement as Laura continued,

"As I recall someone, someone not six feet away from me at the present time, came to my office with a very attractive looking Etruscan bronze bowl they wanted to sell. As was our standard practice in these matters, I examined it, found it genuine and gave a very generous valuation for you. You were selling on behalf of a friend and gave me lots of personal details about your friend. Knowing you as I did, I presumed it was just some creative accounting on your side; I foolishly trusted you. It was sold at auction for a handsome sum."

"Your memory of the events leads me to suspect, even more, that you have revenge on the menu."

"Well, a month later, the bowl came back to the auction house, it was a fake. You switched it somewhere along the line, and the seller, as detailed in the paperwork, did not exist."

"Yes, that was rather mean of me, and I remember when you told them it was me who sold the item, they were very wary of asking me, Mr Mullins, such a trusted and valuable customer. I, of course, denied selling the item. I think I just got carried away, trying something and actually getting away with it."

"I was sacked, they believed that I was defrauding them."

"Which, as you know, you had been doing for a while. You must admit, I was generous once you left, I did share some of the profit with you."

"Money to clear your conscience for screwing a good accomplice over."

"Laura, I am sure you can now see my side of things. This is a perfect opportunity for you to get your revenge. That little thing there might be genuine, until you come back in the morning for your cash, and it has transformed into a worthless replica."

Laura leaned forward and replaced the statue in her bag. She stood up, brushing down her skirt to straighten the creases. "So, you don't want it?"

"Not so fast, I know you are a very intelligent person. Therefore, you understand that to try and get your own back on me, could lead to devastating consequences for you. I do not honestly think that you would risk losing your life, just to get back at me. Also, there is the potential profit I could collect on this transaction; that is a lot of money which I find just too tempting to miss out on. I am banking on the fact that you are not a vindictive person. Come back tomorrow, I will have three hundred thousand pounds in cash for you. As a precaution, I will also have my expert, David, here to ensure you are not going to pass off a fake. I presume I will see you in the morning?"

Laura headed towards the door smiling broadly. She called over her shoulder, "Tomorrow I expect to be offered coffee, you mean old bastard."

Howard laughed loudly, something he rarely did. He stopped when he saw Laura turn back towards him, she stood in the doorway, and pointed at him.

"I seem to recall a story where one of your clients was burgled the night before the deal was competed. Don't think about trying to steal it from me before tomorrow, if you try, you might actually see my vengeful side. And before you ask, yes, I am threatening the great Mr Mullins."

Howard's smile remained, he liked Laura, he liked her a lot.

* * *

"The buyer has agreed to three hundred thousand pounds, Thomas; a result, I would say."

Laura sounded very excited when she rang, something that Thomas was going to change. He had expected her to call in to his shop with the money today, not just to receive a telephone call. He really wanted to speak to her face to face. His concern was simple, would she run if he confronted her? What would her reaction be? He wanted to see her face when he told her he knew exactly how she had acquired the statue. For now, the telephone would have to do, and he did not want to delay.

"I know where that little statue of yours came from." That was all Thomas wanted to say, the simple fact: she had been found out. He half expected her to hang up and he would never hear from her again. He hoped she would not do that, as he wanted to warn her that Gerald was actively looking for her. Gerald, when it came to hitting women, had a reputation for striking out.

She said nothing. He could hear her breathing at the other end of the telephone, if she was going to hang up and disappear, he still wanted to warn her.

"Gerald knows that his marble lady, which was lying next to his decanter, is missing and knows that you have it. Laura, I just want to let you know, Gerald is not a very nice person. If he finds you, I have no doubt he will hurt you."

Laura spoke, "I know exactly what he is like, I did do my homework on him and I know he has one count of common assault against one of his floozies. I'm sure I can handle him. I just didn't know before that you are his dealer."

"What you also didn't know about is another assault that was never reported to the police, that time he just about killed one of his lady-friends. Luckily, I had a very corrupt doctor on my client list, and he helped save her life. It was also fortunate that Gerald had the cash to keep her quiet. I am worried what he might do if he finds you."

"Trust me, I can handle myself, but thanks for the warning. Back to our transaction, it is going to be completed tomorrow. My buyer does not keep the sort of cash we are asking for in the house, so I'll be calling back tomorrow and will be over to see you after lunch. How's that sound?"

Thomas wanted to say more. He wanted to be indignant about the way Laura was handling things and treating him like a lackey. He wanted to ask her what she was really selling the item for, if it was stolen in the first place, but he could not bring himself to ask the question. Part of him said maybe she'll just leave with everything, the other half of him was worried for her safety. So, when he spoke, he tried to sound as convincing as he could.

"You had better show up tomorrow and renegotiate our deal or else it will not just be Gerald looking for you."

He hung up, not like a tough, menacing gangster, but like the foot-soldier he knew he was.

CHAPTER EIGHT THURSDAY LUNCHTIME

Caroline stopped her car in front of Robert's house. When she stepped out, she could see him behind his car loading, what appeared to be, fishing rods into it. She strode up the concrete driveway, he looked up and saw her approaching. Robert looked calm, not despondent as she might have expected, maybe suicide was not on his mind. Not that she knew how anyone might look in the hours before they took their own life. All she knew was Andy sounded concerned and that was enough for her.

He did not greet her, just looked at her coldly, as she stood beside him.

"I need to talk to you about something; can we go inside?"

Robert remained silent, he carefully closed the boot, locked it via the key fob, turned and walked back into the garage. Caroline followed him among the debris of living that clutters garages across the country, then through a door into the main house. They stood in the galley kitchen, facing each other, burnt toast and coffee odours hung in the air. He made no attempt to offer her a seat and seemed to be acting in an ambivalent way towards her.

"I want to explain something to you," she stopped, unsure of how she would clearly describe her predicament. She had not had time to explain to her father that being gay was never going to be a problem to her. She could even forgive him for never trying to contact her or his old family, perhaps because he was ashamed of being gay. Maybe he was ashamed, but no one should ever be, she believed, everyone should be proud of their sexuality. It was just hard if you felt you were in the minority, which Caroline always thought she was, and did not want to be different.

"OK, Caroline," Robert spoke for the first time, "or should I call you 'Peanut'?"

He knew. Caroline was befuddled, how did he know? How long had he known? If Laura had told him, why had he not mentioned it before? Caroline felt a little faint, she held onto the worktop to stop her swaying. The moment you deny who you are, you become lost. So, when the truth comes out, as it always will, people look at you and think, what else are you denying.

"Who told you?"

"Andy forwarded me the last message Laura sent. He has just sent another message. It would seem that you and she had quite a thing going."

Caroline wished she had said something earlier, she had wanted to let everyone know that she was gay, and she was in love. Yet convention had always been a big barrier to her. She had, of course, known Laura when they both worked at the London Auction House, it was there they acknowledged their attraction for each other. During the following few weeks they fell in love and became lovers. Caroline remembered those days with such affection, both her and Laura often recalled them as they lay in each other's arms.

"We are in love."

"Clearly, with the two of you planning to go off and be a couple. Tell me, were you lovers when I first met Laura, when I thought she was just a flatmate to you? Have you always been lovers and was this some sort of crazy scheme to fool a gullible, heterosexual man and have a laugh at his expense?"

"Nothing like that at all," Caroline protested, "it was her idea. You never knew, but her parents threw her out because she was in love with me, that was why she stayed with me, but the flat was so cramped. When she first met you, she liked you, said you were nice and kind. Laura convinced me that living with you for a year or so would give us the chance to save up, get a bigger flat. The alternative would be being stuck in a cramped flat for years."

"Ah, not having a laugh, just taking me for a ride, paying the mortgage and food for her while she was stashing money away for the great gay escape. There was me thinking that Laura was the right one for me. All the time she was leading me along, planning, scheming, then I find out selling some very expensive bit of objet d'art and gathering a large wad of cash in the process. Is there anything else I should know about? Oh, by the way, if her parents had thrown her out, then I imagine her frequent visits to see them was just a cover for the two of you to meet up. What a bitch she has been and what a fool I have been."

Robert banged his fist so hard on the worktop, it made Caroline jump. She could see his point of view. She had never wanted to deceive anyone, it was bad enough for her concealing her sexuality, something she always felt uncomfortable about. Maybe if her father had admitted loudly, all those years ago, that he was gay, he might not have missed Caroline growing up into a young woman and she would not have missed his wisdom and advice. Perhaps then she might have had the confidence not to hide her true feelings and who she really was from the world.

"I once said to Laura that, maybe we should be up front with you, you are a kind person, I was sure you would have helped in some way."

"I am just at a total loss as to how anyone comes up with such a bizarre idea in the first place. Well, it's over now, she has gone from my life and you and your lover will be driving off into the sunset, no doubt laughing all the way and talking about how you duped a stupid man. Hadn't you better be off now and meet up with your lover?"

"That is just the whole point, I have no idea where she is. I have not heard a single word from her since last Thursday. I'm sure something has happened to her; you know that was the reason I came here in the first place."

"I might be naïve, but do not take me for a stupid idiot, she has walked out on me, maybe she planned to run away with you, so maybe she has changed her mind. Laura does not seem to worry about other people's feelings, does she now."

Caroline did not want to hear him speak the words she had often thought over the last week. She had pushed those fears deep down inside her, hoping that they would stay put and not cause her sleepless nights. Laura could be self-centred, she liked to oversee her own destiny. Laura said a lot, but she rarely shared her inner thoughts.

"Would you help me find her, please Robert? The people she has been dealing with are not nice. Our mutual friend found out some disturbing details about Thomas, Gerald and Howard. I just know something has happened to her and I really need your help to find her."

"I used to care Caroline. How blunt do I need to be, I really don't care anymore. If you need a man in your life you should have thought about that before jumping into bed with a woman. Talk to your friend, Andy, he's young and strong, he'll help you uncover what has happened to Laura. Just be aware Caroline, that maybe in the end, she has gone off with a third party and your memories of her will be destroyed, just as mine have been. Now, I want you to leave my house, so I can go off and clear my mind with a spot of fishing. Peace and tranquillity, that is what I need at the moment, time to reflect and time to decide just what I have left in my life."

Caroline left the house, sat in her car and thought about Laura. One of them was the victim and one of them was the survivor. Caroline could not be sure of her role in the situation she found herself in. She had two theories for Laura not contacting her. The one she did not want to consider was that she had come to considerable harm, a victim of one of the men she had been dealing with. She imagined that none of them would be averse to inflicting physical damage to get their hands on a valuable statue. The second theory was that Laura had run away with another person, gone, with no plans to return. In a funny sort of way, that was the theory that Caroline hoped was true. She would much rather think of Laura as being happy and in love, even if she was not the subject of that affection.

Whatever the reason, Caroline had to know it, and the person who should know would be Andy. He must have hacked all Laura's phone records, otherwise Robert would not have known about the last text message. Were there other messages and clues as to another person in her life? Andy could also help find out just who and what the three men Laura was dealing with were doing. Then another thought struck Caroline, Andy could tell when a company share price could be about to go through the roof. The letter that Laura had in her handbag, was she working with him and Gerald to make more money? Caroline remembered that Laura had often 'popped round' to see Andy. Maybe she needed to be a little more wary of Andy.

She looked up, turned on the motor and was about to pull away when she saw Robert drive off in his car, from what he said, to go fishing and 'to decide just what I have left in my life'. Laura had never once mentioned that Robert liked to go angling, not once in the whole year she was with him, had she told Caroline that Robert had gone fishing.

She had rushed down to see Robert, concerned that he was about to follow the pathway of his father. Momentarily, she had forgotten that, she had been pre-occupied with her own demons, wanting to be honest with herself and those around her. Now he was the only thing in her mind, she might not like him, he might not like her, but he was a human being and no human should ever take their own life.

In a decisive split second, she put her own worries about Laura to one side, slammed the car into gear and set off to follow Robert.

* * *

Andy put the phone down after making his request to Caroline to go and see how Robert was. He stared at the table of telephone numbers on his screen. He would have liked to print it out, examine a hard copy, he found that so much easier. When it came to scrutinising data, he was very much old school. However, printing out pages and pages of data would draw attention to himself here in the office where he was surrounded by all his colleagues.

He had not planned to investigate the contents of Laura's mobile telephone at the office among his fellow workers, all going about their endless task of looking into the past and present of people and companies that were on the verge of being awarded a lucrative government contract. It was just that as he browsed her data he had come up with an idea.

After Caroline asked him yesterday about Laura's phone, he thought he would have a poke around the records he could get at. He knew that, without the physical phone, he would only get a partial picture. Earlier, he had located the cellular phone masts that her phone had used as she went around London on the last day that she had been seen. Andy had broadly traced her movements, but he had not yet triangulated the signals which would reveal, to within a few metres, the locations she had visited. His priority was to find out where she might be now. Even a week later, there had not been a single sign of her mobile phone being on anywhere. He could see she was around her home address on

Thursday evening, her phone had remained static until the signal was turned off at ten-eighteen. Maybe her battery had run out, you could never be that sure.

The next time it was turned on was around the Birchington area, which he knew must be the railway station, where he had previously traced her car to. It had been turned on for three minutes and seventeen seconds before it, once again, stopped sending out a signal. No calls had been made at that time, nor was there any web browsing, it appeared to be just turned on then turned off again. It remained off until 4.05am Friday. At that time, it had stayed on for a little over five minutes. The location was close to Canterbury, and again, there were no calls, text messages or web usage.

He tried to picture Laura driving to the station and waiting for someone there, turning her phone on could have been a part of the rendezvous process. Then, with the person she contacted, driving towards Canterbury. Was it then she had got into trouble with that person? Was turning her phone on an attempt to get help before the signal disappeared along with her? He could not be sure of anything.

What Andy really needed was to get into her physical phone, but that was missing. Did she still have it, or had she just dumped it somewhere to avoid anyone tracing her? He did have one last angle he could try. He knew that she used WhatsApp, most of the time, to communicate. If he could gain access to that he would possibly learn a little more about her plans. He also knew her Gmail username. If he could get into that, then just maybe she had left all the defaults in place and her messages would be backed up to the Google email account. He would then be able to see her messages and, hopefully, obtain more clues. It was just a simple password between him and all that data. Data that might help him to locate her.

He had been thinking about the best way to get into it. He had a lot of equipment and computer programmes that might help, but they took time and that meant he risked it being found out that he was doing unauthorised research. He needed to think of what she might have used, most people chose a password that was easy to recall, a birthday, an anniversary, a nickname, something personal.

Sipping his cold coffee, staring at the numbers, he remembered the recent occasion when Laura had called into his flat. It was late and she was after more favours, asking him to dig up yet more information. She apologised for being late: 'Sorry, I stayed with 'Peanut' longer than planned'. Even after some serious bantering from Andy to get her to reveal just who 'Peanut' was, he was told, by a rapturous Laura, it was her special secret. He wondered if it was 'Peanut' that she had met at Birchington.

On a whim, he entered her Gmail details, followed by the password 'Peanut'. He waited for a moment and saw the screen change, Laura's inbox opened up before him. It worked, he was in. Thinking there was no time like the present, he started probing her messages, emails and calls. More importantly, he located the back-up data for her WhatsApp account. It did not take him long to download the file to his own computer, which had the software to open all her messages and media.

He hoped to see some clues which might help to find Laura. Even though he was surrounded by colleagues, he wanted to get answers as quickly as possible and so started reading the messages. He began with the last message, sent to 'Peanut', the special person in Laura's life. It was now clear that she was planning to leave Robert, set off and start a new life with 'Peanut', he just wanted a name for the person. He trawled Laura's contacts to locate the phone number. The message was sent to Caroline Stone. In disbelief, he checked again, had he made a mistake, no, Laura and Caroline were going away together. He flicked through all the 'Peanut' messages, it was clear, the two women were lovers. They had been planning their escape, fooling Robert, taking him for a ride. Without thinking he forwarded the last message to

Robert, as he felt the information needed to be shared with him. He also gave the identity of 'Peanut' to Robert, an action he would later regret. He returned to Laura's messages.

There was a WhatsApp conversation with Robert during that afternoon.

Robert: 'Conference finished, boring as ever, what are you up to?'

Laura: 'Having a lazy Costa coffee.'

Robert: 'Which one?'

Laura: 'The one in the High Street before I go and babysit next door.'

Robert: 'Well enjoy. See you tomorrow. x'

That was the last time that Robert had contacted Laura, Andy felt sorry for his friend. Alright, he thought, Robert was a bit of a bore, always playing by the rules, but he did not need this. His teenage years were so difficult, with first his father taking his own life, then his mother requiring so much care. Andy had hoped that with Laura by his side, Robert might have been able to start to enjoy his life. It now seemed that Robert had, once again, been the victim.

It always gave Andy an uncomfortable feeling, trawling through someone's private messages. Knowing it belonged to Laura only made him feel worse. There were pictures with Robert, without Robert, with Caroline, without Caroline. Pictures of Tower Bridge opening, some unidentified garden, an odd-looking statue, and three or four pictures of her making faces.

Then there were the messages from Caroline, some loving, some brief, some just talking about the day. What was becoming obvious to Andy now was that it was not Caroline she was meeting at Birchington, it was someone else. But who? He needed to ask himself more questions about the little information he had of when she was at Birchington.

He wished he had been a lot more insistent about going with her when she was meeting those men, all of whom were involved with criminal activities. Andy was not blaming himself for her disappearance, but he did feel guilty that he had not done more.

He had found her car parked at Birchington station, her phone signal was picked up close by, as well, so that meant she was there. He looked back at the car park entry and exit records, for no better reason than to re-examine what he already knew. How he had missed it the first time, he had no idea. It was at the top of the list that he had seen Laura's car entering the car park, and when he found that he had not looked any further. Now below, he saw that Laura had gone into the car park earlier and stayed for a few minutes before leaving.

He visualised Laura driving into the car park, staying a short while, before leaving, and then later returning. What was that about. He could not think of any plausible explanation. Had she arrived too early for something.

He could not figure out just why she had turned her phone off at ten-eighteen and then five hours later parked up in Birchington, switched her phone on for only a couple of minutes. Why did she turn her phone on for such a short time? Andy studied the data, no calls, no messages, no web-browsing. More importantly for Andy, the time recorded for the phone communicating with the radio mast was so early in the morning. There were no trains at that time. Birchington Station Car Park had to be a rendezvous point for her. She had to be meeting someone. But why turn the phone on, what would that do? Andy was in difficulty trying to answer that question.

It was a long walk from the train station to Sidcup High Street, which gave Laura plenty of time to consider how she could get around Thomas, now that he knew she had not paid for the figurine, a fact that was going to with rankle him. However, she was confident that she could twist him around her little finger.

She sat in Costa sipping her coffee, her mind reviewing all the probable outcomes with Thomas. Maybe, she could explain to him that it had been her honest intention to buy the figurine from Gerald. Perhaps she should tell him everything, the way she was living with Robert to avoid breaking Caroline's tenancy agreement and that she had had nowhere else to go last year. Also, explain that she and Caroline dreamt of buying a place of their own far away from London, a small flat in Manchester where they could live together and so they had started saving. But then she had found the letter addressed to Gerald and wondered exactly what it meant. When she had asked Andy to do her a favour, give her a bit of background on Gerald Wallace, it had become clear to her the letter was connected to insider share dealing.

Laura had seen an opportunity. If she could convince Gerald to share the knowledge in exchange for still more profit, it would allow her a share and then 'Peanut' and herself would be buying their dream flat a lot more quickly. The first visit he was not convinced of her plan, but Laura had seen the beautiful Cycladic statue beside the decanter, which had taken her breath away. If she could buy it from Gerald and sell it on, then her and 'Peanut's' flat would materialize even sooner. Knowing what she did about Gerald, and the way he had described it as 'tut', she guessed that one hundred thousand pounds would easily get her the figurine and allow her the chance to make a substantial profit when she sold it.

She recalled on her second visit, as she sat there in Gerald's mini mansion, the more she spoke to him, the more she recognised he could be a totally awkward bastard if he wanted to. She knew the instant she suggested purchasing the figure he had disregarded over the years, his greed would have kicked in. Every extra pound he wanted, was one pound less for Laura and 'Peanut'.

It had been from reading the estate agent's description of the two-bedroom duplex, which sounded perfect, that Laura had known it was just the place to live and love and she wanted it for her 'Peanut'. It had not been a quick decision to make, as she sat and spoke to Gerald about the share dealing, she wondered; should she steal it, just take it, or open the conversation towards buying the figurine? This addled old man would not miss it, then she could tell Thomas she had bought it, he would never know. With the hundred thousand pounds Thomas had given her, plus her share of the profits, the flat was now in touching distance. She took the statue on impulse. She now needed to somehow get around Thomas.

Now all the parts of the jigsaw seemed to be falling into place, maybe not perfectly, but they were piecing themselves together. Laura wanted to call 'Peanut', let her know their shared savings would increase dramatically over the next twenty-four hours.

"I told you it would all work out; the buyer has agreed the price I asked for. We can sit down together at the weekend and choose which flat we want to live in. I still like the duplex I told you about, did you have the chance to see it on-line......Yes the post office one.......I know it looks really good......Well we can't just walk in with cash and buy it, you can't do that anymore, there are so many money laundering rules around now. But we can get a mortgage, not a large one....... We can put a fair-sized deposit down, then drip-feed the cash into our accounts to avoid any suspicion......Of course it will work, trust me."

As she spoke, Laura became aware that someone was taking the seat next to her, she turned to see who it was.

"'Peanut', I have got to go now; love you."

She had not planned on seeing that Cheshire cat grin ever again.

Gerald Wallace grabbed her wrist and held it so tightly his fingers turned white.

"I guess you are a little surprised to see me join you."

"Let go of me."

"Now-now, bitch, I want everyone to think I am your kindly uncle taking you for afternoon tea, and not about to break your wrist, the first of many bones in your body I plan to break until you give me back what is rightfully mine." He placed his foot on hers and pressed down hard. "Remember, that little statue thing. I know you have it, plus a rather large amount of money that you borrowed to buy it. You are a very naughty girl. Unfortunately, not the sort of naughty I like."

"Or pay for."

"You have been caught. So, where is that little reclining lady and the money someone sent you out to buy it with, although, in the end, you stole it."

She was uncomfortable, anxious about the situation she found herself in, but for all that, it was her father she saw next to her, inflicting pain and asking the same question.

'You little bugger, you stole 'em. Don't fucking lie, our corner shop Indian popped in and mentioned he thought you might be stealing. So, what you doin' with the money: smoking?' Her father twisted the skin on her wrist further, she was ten years old, however much she tried, she could not stop the tears of pain from rolling down her cheeks. She had been caught out.

The ten-year-old Laura thought it was an easy scam. Her mother gave her some money to 'pop down' to the shop and pick up some groceries. Laura just stole to order and kept the money. It was going to be her escape fund to buy herself some nice dresses and a rail ticket to anywhere. No matter how disabled her father might be, he could still find ways of inflicting pain.

"If I have to leave here with you and walk outside, the pain will be greater for you," Gerald threatened. "Where is it?"

As a ten-year-old, Laura just accepted the beating she knew she was going to get for stealing. She would get a thrashing for dropping plates when she washed up, spilt drinks or forgot to bring her father his favourite cup. 'Laura, get yer arse in here'. Dutifully, she would walk towards her father and stand close to him, that was the way it had to be. She was first admonished, then grabbed and then thrashed.

Today Laura no longer accepted being told what to do.

"Take your hands and foot off me Gerald, or else there will be a scene."

"You have no idea just how nasty I can be to a woman, no matter how pretty she is."

Laura looked into his eyes, his breath stroking her face.

"I know exactly how you treat women. Have you forgotten I know all about your past, your share dealing, your common assault on a prostitute? You do realise that I know you purchase class A drugs for weekends with paid-for escorts. More importantly, I know you almost killed a woman, a fact that was never officially reported to the police." She felt his grip loosen just a little. "Luckily you have some friends who patched her up for you, then you paid her a large amount of money to keep quiet. I know so much about you, I guess it would only take one telephone call to see you behind bars again."

"Idle threats."

"Want to see how idle I can be? I guess you prefer your freedom to having a nondescript figurine on your table. Let me tell you how this all plays out. You are going to let go of me and I am going to stand up and walk away from here, leaving you behind. You can then put this down to a bad experience with a woman. Plus, you can be thankful you still have your freedom. Oh, and if you're wondering just how I know about this," Laura wanted to protect Thomas, she had no real reason to, she just felt it was the right thing to do. "The police hold all sorts of different types of intelligent reports, it turns out the 'bent' doctor is a bit of an informer. Luckily for you, you were able to pay off the girl. So, are you going to let me go now?"

Gerald looked at her for a few seconds, he was clearly thinking about his options. Laura guessed he did not have many, if any.

"Let us not forget that you are a common thief, who stole a very valuable item from my house. When you visited me to talk about insider dealing, which I turned down because I am no longer dishonest, out of frustration, you stole from under my nose a family heirloom, a valued belonging of my late father. Then there is the small matter of your second theft, from an innocent antiques dealer, a large sum of money. Two can play at blackmail and I think mine works best. Now, where is the statue?"

Laura had a final card to play, although she was not sure that what she was going to share with Gerald was fact. It had been based partly on what Andy had told her, a vague rumour, as Andy put it: 'there is no smoke without fire and the man has form'. She had supplemented that rumour to what she had seen, hoping it would add up correctly.

"There is one more story I think I should share with you. It started back in two thousand and two, when an American, Marc Dreier, started selling promissory notes to hedge funds and investors. The problem was the notes were fake, a classic Ponzi Scheme. Aided by friends of his impersonating real people to drag more investors in. He even had an agent based in the U.K. receiving phone calls and impersonating British hedge funds, convincing still more gullible investors to put their hard-earned cash into Dreier's crooked scheme."

Laura felt the grip on her wrist relax, she was on the right track, so continued with more confidence.

"So, the authorities over here, once the whole sorry business came to light, started to look around for the 'impersonator' to extradite to the U.S. They had a name but not much proof.

"While Dreier was in prison awaiting trial, one of his conspirators popped into the office and stole two valuable paintings. See, who can you trust in the financial world? They got the conspirators, but not the paintings, both by Thomas Eakins. If you're interested in what they look like, then I suggest you have a close look at the two you have hanging in your study."

Gerald released his grip, allowing Laura to stand and leave him just as she had instructed. She did hear the words he spoke as she walked away.

"There are better places for me to deal with you. Best lock your door tonight, Sweetie. Dead whores never tell tales."

* * *

"Is he up yet?" Sheila asked as she placed the single shopping bag on the kitchen worktop. Laura walked in from the living room to greet her.

"Yes, about five minutes after you went shopping, he called out, so I brought him down and put him in front of the television, he seemed happy enough."

"I hope I haven't put you out too much, it was just that I wanted a couple of things from the shop. I suppose I am being silly, but I hate leaving him on his own, even if he is having his afternoon nap. As it turns out, I'm glad I asked you to look after him, it put my mind at rest."

"He's no trouble, Sheila, you know I like coming in and helping out."

Laura did feel a little guilty. Saturday she would be leaving this area and starting her new life with 'Peanut'. Not having the chance to say a proper goodbye to Sheila or her husband; would they understand. Sheila might, if she knew all the circumstances of Laura's life. Her husband, she doubted, was aware of much that went on around him. He might not even notice that she no longer called in.

When Sheila asked her to stay for a cup of tea, Laura found it hard to refuse. She planned to pop in briefly tomorrow morning, unannounced, then that would be it, no time for tea and chat then. Laura sat down as Sheila busied herself with the kettle.

"I know you like fruit teas, so I thought I'd try out a new one on you. They call it one of those detoxing teas that are meant to be good for you. If I really knew what detox was, I might agree, but I thought I would try it anyway."

"I just like the variety of infusions that you can get, I think they are healthier for you rather than all that caffeine in tea and coffee."

Laura looked at Sheila as she placed two mugs on the table, one had a heart shape on it, the other was for some building company which Laura had never heard of.

142

"Not like you to use mugs, unless you are getting to be like us young people?"

"More practical, he can hold a mug a bit easier, plus if he drops it, it does not cost as much to replace."

"But you can hold a cup and saucer," Laura joked.

"Yes, but I don't like to treat him any differently," Sheila sounded a little serious.

They talked about nothing much, the weather, the neighbours at number six who have had another baby, Mrs Williams who might have to go to hospital for her cataract. As Laura listened, she thought about her departure, packing her bags and moving on. She wondered what Sheila might think, if she told her the reasons and who she was leaving Robert for. Laura hoped that after the weekend she would not have to move on again or be trapped somewhere that she did not want to be. She wanted her love for 'Peanut' to last forever and 'Peanut', in turn, to love her forever.

"So, any plans for the weekend?" Sheila asked, as if somehow, she had read Laura's mind.

"Going to see my parents at the weekend, back on Monday," Laura used the same lie she had told to Robert, somehow repeating the falsehood made the act a lot easier.

"You often go to see them but never really talk much about them."

"There is not a lot to talk about, they are just Mum and Dad, nothing special. They brought me into the world, looked after me and then let me go into the big world on my own." Laura wished it had been that simple. It might have been, but for an IRA bomb, she could still have been living with them. That explosion had not only blown her father apart, it had rippled through her life, pushing her away from the father she might, in different circumstances, have loved.

The infusion had now cooled a little, Laura sipped the liquid, she grimaced.

"Ugh, that is a weird flavour, what's in it?"

"Well, they say fennel is the main ingredient, but there are all different things in it," Sheila sipped her tea. "Well, as you say, there are a lot of flavours in there, but as my mum used to say: 'if it tastes bad then it must be good for you'."

"And we say, our mums know best, so we drink it."

"Not just Mums, older friends like me. I say the same to him in there, watching the TV, if I am trying to get him to take some medicines, and he tries to push me away. I make him drink it in the end. Once, I made him ginger and garlic tea for a cold he had, he hated it, but that cold soon went. You can't beat herbal remedies; all that natural stuff must be good for you, far better than lots of man-made chemicals."

"I do agree with you, although sometimes I suspect that some of these herbal remedies are made to taste deliberately bad. I'm sure if they all tasted yummy, none of us would believe they were going to do us any good at all."

Sheila took a sip of tea, then said, "You should really always keep in touch with your parents. I know from my own experience, that when they have gone, you regret not spending more time with them, I know I do. The problem is we see our parents as those people who stopped us having fun and doing the things we wanted to when we were young. But when we get older, well, we see that they were just doing their best for us. Have they ever visited you here?"

"No, but I take your point. Although you have never met my parents," Laura smiled wryly, as she imagined her father and Sheila having a very tense conversation. She took another mouthful of the strong-tasting fluid, the flavour was not so bad the second time, her taste buds were becoming accustomed to it.

As Laura finished her tea, she realised, for the first time, that as she walked out of Sheila's and returned to her own house to pack her weekend case, her new life was actually starting. There would be no turning back now. Once the case was packed with just the bare essentials, her new journey with Caroline would start. Tonight, would be her last night in Robert's house and she still had things to do before the evening was out, so she had better get started.

"Well, I hope I'm better for that. I'd best be going now; I'll see you next week."

Laura knew that she would not see Sheila next week, she would see her only one more time. Tomorrow morning, she wanted to make an unexpected visit, for some lame excuse, maybe telling Sheila that she had lost an earring. All she wanted was three minutes alone in the bedroom, then she would be free and away from Sidcup forever.

Having spoken to Sheila about parents, something inside Laura churned over and over. She looked at her watch. Her mother was not young, she was not really that well. Up until last year, she had always been close to her mother, 'comrades-in-arms' against the foe by the fireplace, that was once how her mother had described their relationship, they laughed until the tears tumbled from their eyes. Laura could not just leave without saying goodbye, face to face. She decided, more out of guilt than anything else, that she wanted to see her mother just one more time before she left. Unfortunately, that would mean having to see and probably speak to her father, but for her mother's sake she would endure that. She jumped into her small, white Fiat and drove across town towards their bungalow.

* * *

Laura looked down into her mother's eyes, they were tired and frail; they had lost the sparkle of a young mother. She was still her mother. A mother to both a daughter and a broken old man. There must have been a time when her mother loved her father, looked upon him with wonderment, but now Laura was not so sure her mother felt the same.

"Laura," was all her mother could say at first, her voice tremulous with emotion. Laura said nothing, she just hugged her mother tightly, she could feel bones through her thin dress, she had lost weight since the last time Laura had seen her. She knew her mother had always been a worrier, wanting to do everything for everyone, without any regard for her own wellbeing.

"It's so good to see you, darling. Come in, get your coat off. How long can you stay?"

Laura followed her ageing mother into the house. They stopped in the kitchen doorway, her mother looking undecided what to do with her daughter.

"I'm so pleased to see you, dear."

"Well, I can't stay that long, I have really just come to see you and say a proper goodbye before I move up to Manchester. I felt guilty having sent just a letter telling you I was going, so here I am."

"You needn't have worried yourself; I got the letter and Mrs Dodds next door read it to me as my eyes are not what they used to be. I'm so happy for you. Pleased that you have someone to love you, that is so important, without being loved, what is the point of living."

"You really must take better care of yourself, Mum. When was the last time you had an eye test?"

Laura's mother shuffled uncomfortably, "I have been meaning to get 'round to it."

"Well, see you do. As you might have guessed from the letter, I wasn't planning to come, but it wasn't that I didn't want to see you, I was just avoiding him in there." Laura flicked her eyes towards the living room, where she knew her father would be sitting in his chair.

Her mother stepped closer and whispered, "He's more than likely trying to listen to us now."

They smiled at each other, sharing another moment of warm comradeship, a solidarity that bonded them against a common foe.

As if on cue, their antagonist called out from his chair, "Who yer yapping with, Mother?"

Laura observed the frown that now washed across her mother's face, that moment of warmth had flowed away and was now flooded with trepidation. Laura knew that her mother lived with a man who kept her in a constant state of tension. Laura smiled comfortingly, trying to calm her mother, then turned and walked purposefully towards the living room, her mother following her timidly.

"Your daughter has come to say hello and ask how her father is," Laura proclaimed.

"What do yer want 'ere?"

"I just told you, I've come to see how you are."

She saw the familiar sour look on his face and wondered if her father ever smiled. She could not recall ever seeing him smile or laugh. She wondered if the I.R.A had blown his smile from him as well.

"Yer' never bothered yerself before, trying to make up to me?"

Laura pulled up and sat on a small wooden stool with a worn upholstered seat. It was the same one, she recalled, that she used to climb on and jump off, imagining she was diving into a warm blue lagoon in the middle of a tropical rain forest. Then she had been either five or six years old, her mother fussed around telling her to be careful. All the while she played, her father kept telling her to 'shut up, I'm watching telly.'

"No," she replied, "just wanted to say I am moving up to Manchester with my friend, so you might not see so much of me."

"Why Manchester, you do know that it is a shit 'ole. All smoke and factories, unemployment like you wouldn't believe and it is always raining. You are stupid even to think about going there let alone living up there. Why bother moving anyway, just a waste of time, paying out on lawyers and estate agents, all after yer money. Bloody vultures they are, money, money, money. They'll charge you a hundred pounds just to answer a bloody simple question."

"Dad, you haven't even been to Manchester, so how come you know so much about it?"

"I read the papers, yer know, and they don't paint a pretty picture of the north I can tell yer."

"Well, anyway I'm going to live in Manchester which is a very modern forward-thinking city, full of fun and night life, something else you don't know too much about." She had not meant to taunt him; it was something she could not help herself doing.

"I know that's where yer type go and live. It's a city of dykes, that's why I never wanted to go up there, with all your sort there, it'll be even worse than a shit 'ole. But if you must go, then bugger off and leave me to fend for meself. Don't worry about yer old dad, I'll get by."

Laura stood up from the small stool and pushed it away from her. She noticed her mother standing nervously in the doorway, watching the conversation develop into a confrontation, as it always did, ever since Laura had admitted to her parents that she was gay and in love.

"Fend for yourself? When have you ever been alone long enough to have to fend for yourself? Mother is at your beck and call all day every day. I gave you the best years of my life, years I can never get back, just to look after you and attend to your every whim. But now I must go and live some years for myself, before those years catch up on me and I find myself in a chair waiting to die. At that point I want to have some pleasant memories to look back on. Just because you have wallowed in your own self-pity, you have no right to inflict that misery on everyone around you."

Her father threw his newspaper onto the floor at the side of his chair, the tabloid pages parting and covering the threadbare, stained carpet. He turned, as best he could, towards his daughter, spit coming from his mouth as he shouted at her,

"People have no idea just what it's like to be 'alf a man. Sitting here knowing I can never be a real bloke, never go back to having both legs and both hands. Day in and day out I sit here, the only thing I have to look forward to is fucking death. I could have died in Northern Ireland fighting for my country, instead I am now stuck in a living hell."

"Don't twist the truth," Laura raised her voice, anger rising inside her, "you had every chance to have false limbs fitted, the army gave you loads of opportunities to rehabilitate and live a near normal life. You're not the only soldier to leave his legs on the battlefield; you just enjoy being a burden to everyone, a martyr, getting everyone to feel sorry for you. The only reason you have nothing to look forward to is because you have given up on yourself. You are the only person stopping you.

Mother and I, to you, are just collateral damage in a war that you are still fighting inside your head."

"If I could get out of this chair, I'd give you a good thrashing my girl. It's yer mother who put all these mad ideas in your stupid head, going off, leaving us. Your duty is here my girl, with your parents, not off living the life of a pervert, kissing girls. No sense of duty, that's the problem with the young, shirking responsibility, that's all you know. So just fuck off and leave us."

"Best leave him," Laura's mother advised from the doorway. When Laura was younger, she would have taken the advice but not anymore, instead she shouted back at her father,

"Have you ever considered that other people have a life, a point of view that might be different to yours. I'm different, I love a woman and the woman I love makes me a whole person. Being different should be celebrated and, in the same way, your disability should be embraced, all of us should do the best we can. Be proud. I'm proud to be gay, you should be proud to be disabled."

"I'm proud to be a war veteran but I'm not proud to have a daughter like you. I wish you'd never been born; you've always been trouble, always been a bitch of a daughter."

Laura's voice lowered; she spoke as if she was having a normal conversation, "And you're the father from hell," was her next contribution to the argument.

Her father shuffled on his chair, his only hand sliding under the worn cushion he sat on. He lifted to one side. Both his wife and daughter looked at him, wondered what he was trying to achieve. Then he pulled something out from underneath him, he brought his hand up, pointing it at Laura, in it he held a large revolver; Laura had never seen the weapon before.

"Always keep a gun close by, good advice from 'the Troubles', now fuck off and never come back or else I pull the fucking trigger."

"You mustn't hurt Laura," her mother pleaded

"Mustn't I, says who?" he sneered.

CHAPTER NINE THURSDAY LUNCHTIME

Caroline followed Robert onto the M2. He was not driving fast or erratically, he was just steady, he appeared not to be in any kind of rush. The traffic was light and soon Caroline's mind began to wander and wonder.

She wondered why her father had not tried to contact her at all. Had he really been content to live his life, knowing he had a daughter growing up somewhere? Was he that ashamed of being gay? Maybe he was. Caroline recognised she was just the same as him, not wanting to admit that she was gay. Not admitting something that comprises everything you do, it holds you back, leads you to make the wrong decisions. She now regretted that she had agreed to Laura going to live with Robert, just because they wanted to save for a place of their own. She was sure she could have requested an amendment to her tenancy agreement, which would have allowed them to both live there, despite its small size, they could have managed. If not, they could have found somewhere else. They could have rented a small flat where they could live happily together, then it would not have mattered how long it took them to buy a place of their own. The truth was that Caroline was ashamed of what other people might say or think of two women living together, so, Laura had left her for Robert.

If her father had come back to see her, explain that he was gay, then maybe she could have admitted her sexuality openly. But perhaps she was not sure of it herself. Living with just her mother and stepfather, she, as a young girl, had always helped around the pub. The regulars, she had known since she was a small girl, began to see her as a young teenage woman, with whom they flirted and pawed, to the amusement of her stepfather. It came to the point where she was frightened to go downstairs into the bar. Her mother just put it down to harmless fun with the customers, but Caroline could not see it that way and her fear of those men drinking in the bar extended to the boys of her own age who just liked her. Maybe she was not gay at all. Maybe it was just that she could not feel relaxed in the company of a man and it was just other women that she could feel comfortable with, not feel threatened. Was that being gay or just clinging to something you were not afraid of? That thought worried her. Laura was not shy to talk about the boyfriends she had at a time when she was not sure who she was, uncertain of her own sexuality. And Laura had lived with Robert for a year, shared his bed, shared his life, had they developed some sort of relationship?

Caroline wanted to scream. She could make no sense of what was happening around her. She began to fear that she was never meant to have more than one significant person in her life. Her father had arrived, so Laura must leave.

Robert turned off the M2 towards the Thanet coast, the directional signs indicated that Birchington was getting closer.

Laura's car, Howard Mullins, now Robert, why was Birchington at the centre of all this. Caroline took a deep breath, put her own fears to one side, concentrating on where Robert might lead her. She began to suspect it was not going to be to his suicide.

* * *

Andy kept asking himself the same question again and again. Why would you decide to turn on your phone at 2.47am in a deserted station car park, make no calls, not send any messages, then turn it off at 2.50am. If Laura had turned her phone off to avoid being traced, then why turn it on at all? Andy racked his brain, looked at his own phone, turned it off then turned it on again, hoping it might inspire him. It did.

Andy thought there must have been some sort of information on the phone that Laura wanted badly enough to risk being traced. It was a hunch, but Andy went back to his computer and checked Laura's bank account. She was always a little forgetful and she must have forgotten her pin number, as he could see that at 2.52am, she withdrew one hundred pounds from the ATM located beside Birchington Station.

Which raised another question. Why did she need one hundred pounds at that time of the morning?

Once again Andy tried to put himself into her shoes. She wanted to escape, that was becoming clear to him. She planned to leave her car behind, so she needed transport. Unless she met someone there in the car park, she needed a cab which could not be traced. She used her phone briefly again later near Canterbury. Again, no call, no mobile data used, just turned on and off again.

Now it was beginning to make sense to him. She parked at the station, turned her phone on, knowing it could be traced. Then grabbed a cab to take her towards Canterbury, where she once again switched her phone on hoping to lay a false trail. She could then change cabs and go to the rendezvous place to join her other man or woman. He needed to find that first cab.

He traced and called the nearest cab companies. There were just three, none of which admitted to doing a cash job at that early hour on Friday morning. He needed to cast his net further from the station.

The room was silent, in fact the whole house was quiet, only Laura disturbed it as she flopped down onto Robert's sofa. For the first time in her life, she had thought she was going to die. Her father pointing a gun at her, which she found out was loaded when he fired it. She had closed her eyes tightly, waiting for the pain, or whatever the feeling is when you are shot. All she heard was her mother scream and the sound of breaking glass, as the bullet went through the glass of a picture that had hung on the wall for as long as she could recall.

Her father had dropped the gun to the floor and started sobbing like a child. Her mother rushed towards him and held him close. Laura watched and was astounded at how deep and forgiving love can be. She left them, embracing, crying. They had no need of anyone but each other. However warped their life together might seem from the outside, it worked for them.

Her heart was still beating fast, even now that she was back in Robert's house. A place where she had always considered herself to be a guest. A convenient stopping point, while she prepared the foundation for her life with 'Peanut'. A new life, away from everything that had hurt her in the past. Her father, the shady dealings at the London Auction House, helping Howard and others make unscrupulous profit from innocent customers. Her new life would be clean, untainted, ordinary and simple. Just her and 'Peanut'.

She laid back on the sofa, wallowing in the silence that she enjoyed so much. Robert always insisted on having music on everywhere in the house. She hated it but accepted it; a small price to pay for escaping London. She stood up, walked to the kitchen and poured herself a glass of milk. She had heartburn. The fear and the threats of the day had taken their toll on her fragile stomach. She drank down the soothing fluid, it was time to pack her weekend case. This was going to be her last night here.

Standing there alone in the kitchen, her ears detected the slightest of sound. A Yale lock turning, then the unmistakable sound of a metal hinge moving as a door opened. The front door was opening. As if to confirm her apprehension, she thought she felt a breath of cold air, or was it just a shiver of fear embracing her.

Silently, she placed the glass on the worktop, then carefully and slowly opened the drawer nearest to her. All the time she listened. A footstep in the hall. Her hand fumbled around the drawer and latched onto a large knife. She heard a gentle sound as the front door closed. Someone else was in the house. Robert was not due back until tomorrow. A stranger's steps grew louder, somebody else was in the house. What did they want? The statue? She knew exactly what Howard was like, why pay out any money when something can get taken in a simple burglary. She gripped the handle of the knife tightly. Then another thought, had Gerald come to see her, had he found out her address somehow? He might want to hurt or even kill her. Again, her heart was racing, she could not stop the trembling in her hands as she held the knife in front of her, her only line of defence against the footsteps that were getting closer and closer.

CHAPTER TEN THURSDAY AFTERNOON

Lady Luck always looked after Henry the Hulk. He liked the nickname that people had given him, it made him feel special. All through his life he had got himself into scrapes, but Lady Luck had always seen him through those scrapes. It also helped that he was well over six-foot-tall, powerfully built, with firm, strong muscles. It was his strong arms and powerful legs that had earned him a small fortune as a hod-carrier in his younger days. The money back then had come far too easily, it had also departed his pockets too easily.

Henry liked the horses and thought he understood them better than most. It turned out the bookies knew even more than he did about horse racing. Then there were the constant jibes at work. Building workers liked to show off, be seen to be tough and real men. Even though he was bigger than most of the men there, he was still taunted for having extremely large front teeth, which gave him a broad grin. He took most in good humour, until one day, a short, outspoken, Irish welder told Henry he could do him a favour and weld his mouth shut, 'we'll not see your bloody fangs or hear the shite you spurt out any longer.'

On a normal day, Henry might have just shrugged his shoulders, offered some verbal abuse back and then returned to moving bricks. On that fateful day, he had lost the best part of a month's money on a stupid grey horse at Newmarket. He punched the welder until his Irish face was no more than a bloody pulp.

Henry lost his job and gained six months bed and board at Brixton Prison.

Upon his release he did several boring building jobs, nothing more than a simple labourer, working for a mere pittance . The wages could not cover his gambling. To help with the gambling, he and a friend carried out a simple armed robbery at a local post office. His unusual teeth, heavy build and criminal record all contributed to the police taking just three days to knock on his door. This time he had seven years bed and board.

Henry still thought Lady Luck was working on his side. Being caught and getting a long sentence meant he had little chance to gamble. Also, he became friends with a very posh, well-educated man who dealt in antiques. He was a kind man with glasses, who everyone said looked like Heinrich Himmler. Henry didn't know who Himmler was, he guessed that he must have been a kind person, as the man with the glasses promised him a job when Henry was finally released.

True to his word, Henry went straight from prison to the house of Mr Howard Mullins, where he stayed and worked. Henry was happy to do many of the household chores, including some cooking, chauffeuring, even cleaning and moving furniture around, plus a little decorating when needed. For the most part, he just had to stay close to Mr Mullins, in case his strength was needed to offer the intimidation of violence to anyone who upset Mr Mullins.

Hearing his name being called, Henry walked into the kitchen where Mr Mullins added, "Come here, I have a job for you."

Henry wondered if he was going to need to inflict some pain or just fear into the man who was sitting next to Mr Mullins. Henry thought that was unlikely as the man called Thomas often popped in and Henry was aware that they had some sort of business arrangement. Just what that arrangement was, Henry had never asked or would dream of asking.

"Henry, here's the address of a Caroline Stone. I need you to find her and invite her to share with you just where Laura, the lady with the statue I was going to buy, is now living. There is a chance that they will be at the same address, as they were planning to elope. I should point out Henry, they are lovers, so she might not be very keen on sharing anything with you. However, I'm sure you can be very persuasive. I would encourage you to get onto this pronto, I have a lot of money at stake."

Henry liked it when Mr Mullins allowed him to handle things his way. It made him feel trusted and he knew that Mr Mullins did not trust many people at all.

As Henry arrived outside the address Mr Mullins had given him, he recognised Caroline as he saw her jump into a car and drive away; Henry followed. While he trailed her car through the streets of south London, to be sure he was doing the right thing, he checked in with Mr Mullins. Mr Mullins sounded pleased.

When Henry was younger, life had seemed very simple. He did not like the modern days, with girls loving girls and men having babies, things just did not seem right to him. He was thankful he had never got involved with anyone, he had kept his life simple and avoided relationships.

It was about half an hour later that he saw Caroline park outside a house on the outskirts of Sidcup and walk up the driveway towards a man beside a car. Henry was sure it was the same man she had been with when she had visited Mr Mullins. He decided that he had best wait, it would be better if she was alone when he asked about Laura. He waited and watched for another fifteen minutes before she came out and walked back to her car. A moment or two later, he saw the man get into his car and drive away; Caroline followed him. Henry joined the convoy; maybe they would all be going to see Laura, now that would please Mr Mullins.

Henry looked at his fuel gauge, he hoped they would not be going too far, he had maybe a hundred miles or so of diesel left. He should have filled up yesterday, if he lost them Mr Mullins would shout at him. So, when he saw the signs for Birchington, Henry was a little relieved, they appeared to be heading for the seaside, even if they drove on to Ramsgate, he would still have enough fuel.

He followed, sometimes a little too close he worried, but he was still behind Caroline. He was now in an area he knew well. Every weekend he was here with his master, enjoying a lazy couple of days. They passed the station, turned right onto Epple Bay Avenue and continued until turning left into Sea Road.

The man's car parked first, then Caroline drove past and parked further along Sea Road; Henry did the same. He looked in his rear-view mirror to see the man take out what appeared to be fishing rods from his car boot and proceed to walk back towards the town. Caroline followed him.

Henry got out of his car, zipped up his jacket to protect himself from the biting wind that came off the sea. He leaned on the sea wall where he was able to easily observe them both.

* * *

However much Caroline tried to fit the pieces together, she could not form a clear, focussed picture in her mind, there were still too many variables swirling around her head. Instead, she concentrated on following Robert as he drove into Birchington, passed the railway station and the car park where Laura had left her car the week before, and turning right onto a residential road, lined on both sides with parked cars, the houses different in shape and size. This was no purpose-built housing estate; it was a road that had grown organically as the town flourished.

It was a long, narrow road and Robert was driving slowly, often stopping to allow oncoming cars to pass. This gave Caroline the time to think some more, recall conversations she had forgotten. She remembered a conversation, from over a year ago, at the time Laura had arrived at her door, with just a small suitcase, asking to stay for a few days. That was all she needed, she said, 'a few days'. Why a few days? That was the question, Caroline asked herself. Laura had left her parents' house for good, she had no plans, or did she? It was only a week later that she had brought Robert into the flat after their adventure in the broken-down lift. After that he often popped in. They talked about their childhoods and Robert talked about the many days he had spent beside the sea during the school holidays. He loved Birchington. She now clearly recalled him smiling, telling Laura, herself and Andy, as they sat sharing a bottle of wine, how he would spend hours swimming and walking along the coast there.

A dark picture began to emerge in Caroline's mind. Laura leaving her car at the station and walking along this very road, in the early hours of the morning, towards a new address, where she might now be waiting for Robert to arrive.

As Robert continued to drive, that scenario became redundant. He left the houses behind and parked on a road that ran along the cliff edge. She drove past and parked a little further ahead of his car. She watched as he pulled his fishing rods out of his car then walked back along the path, towards the town. Caroline stepped out into the cold wind. Was he just innocently going fishing? Besides the two of them, Caroline noticed another car parked further up the road, close to some houses. A resident coming home after shopping perhaps. All she knew was this was a quiet location to park. On a warm, sunny day, it would have been the ideal place for a walk along the coast. Today, she had to risk Robert seeing her.

She followed him from what she hoped was a safe distance. He seemed to be walking, unaware and unworried about his surroundings. About thirty yards from his car, he began to descend, walking down stone stairs which took him onto the rocks that covered the shoreline. She remained standing at the top of the stairs, as he carefully scrabbled and slipped across the algae-covered rocks. Carefully, she followed him, convinced that he would at any time turn around and see her alone on the rocks. But for the two of them, the area appeared deserted. The cliffs, small as they were, had been eroded and shaped following years of tides crashing against them. The dark patches on the cliffs were caves, drilled out by the sea water searching out every weakness in the crags.

He stopped in front of one of the caves and turned to look around. Caroline ducked down between two slippery rocks, grazing her ankle, and smearing her trousers with a green slime. Her heart raced; she gave herself a few seconds, then carefully peered over her veil of rock. Robert had disappeared.

Cautiously, she worked her way towards the point she had last seen him. At the entrance to the cave, she saw his discarded fishing rods. She moved carefully as she made her way to the opening to the cave. She could see nothing. She crouched over, edging forward into the darkness. She heard a voice, Robert's, speaking to someone deep in the cave darkness.

"You look surprised to see me again."

THURSDAY ONE WEEK EARLIER.

"You look as though you've just seen a ghost."

"Shit, Robert, I wasn't expecting you until tomorrow; I thought we had burglars."

Robert walked towards Laura, he kissed her on the forehead. He noticed she had a glass of milk, but he was not going to ask, he no longer cared that much.

"I had a call, so thought I had better come back. Shame to miss out on the vinyl fair, maybe next time."

"Work called you back, that's unlike them."

"Not work, someone called Gerald Wallace," he turned his back and walked into the living room as he spoke to her. He wanted to shout at her, instead he managed to suppress the pressure that was building inside him and spoke calmly, "I think you might know Mr Wallace quite well; he clearly knows you, he was very keen to discover where you might be hanging out this afternoon."

"You know Gerald?"

Robert could hear the tremor in her voice. She looked flushed as she walked in front of him and faced him. Oh yes, Robert thought, I know him well. Well enough to be surprised that your skin is not bruised as a result of the clear rage that Gerald was feeling, when he called me to ask for help to find a Laura Evans. That had shocked Robert, he soon learnt the reason, he just wanted to hear it from Laura.

"Yes, he's a good friend I have known for a couple of years. He called me, asked if I knew where you were, apparently you have something of his. He was most upset. Haven't you spoken to him yet?"

"You called and asked me where I was, you bastard, you told him where to find me."

"Maybe you should have been a bit quicker having your coffee, a taxi from town to here takes a while, you could have missed him altogether. I'm surprised he didn't convince you to return his silly, little statue."

"He's not getting it back, he is a bully, a rich bully who treats women like shit. He deserves everything he fetes."

"I think you mean everything 'he gets'. Have you been drinking?" Robert could not smell any alcohol on her breath, nevertheless she was slurring her words, maybe it was fear because she had been caught out.

"Tell me, why do you know him, and why did he call you?"

"Laura, you know what I do, I have access to shed loads of information on people. He just turned to me to help find a petty crook, *thankfully he does not know we are partners. I helped, why not? So why steal his bloody stupid statue in the first place and why the hell did you pick on him, given the number of people in London you could steal from."*

"It's you, isn't it?" She flopped down onto the sofa, pulled a tissue from a box beside her and wiped her lips.

"What do you mean 'it's me'?"

"Giving Gerald inside information about which shares are going to rocket as soon as it is announced that they are getting a lucrative government contract."

Robert turned towards her, his look had changed, a look of rage was imprinted across his face. The pressure within him was now starting to release, his voice was louder.

"What are you talking about? I'm talking about you walking into someone's house and stealing." Robert hadn't believed Gerald as he shouted and ranted about this woman, Laura Evans, stealing a figurine that was worth a lot of money, as well as trying to blackmail him about the share dealing. How could anyone know? He had been meticulous in ensuring that nothing he did was traceable. Gerald and he only communicated by written letter, which they agreed would be destroyed once the shares had been bought. Robert was all too aware of how easy it was to trace electronic communications.

"Don't act all innocent, Robert, I know what you have been up to, making a lot of money sharing valuable information with your friend. Funny you've never mentioned him before. Maybe he was a friend that you searched out in that wonderful database of yours, find some crooked share dealer, offer him an arrangement he would jump at. So, don't get up on your high horse about stealing. You're doing the same thing."

"Gerald told me you were asking him about a letter as well. Where did you find it?"

"It was caught up in the morning dew, stuck on the driveway. I thought it odd and guessed it might be something to do with you, I just needed someone to confirm my suspicions. Gerald never did."

"So why didn't you just ask me? So much simpler."

"Given that you were doing something illegal, I couldn't see you just admitting to it. Stealing is a crime."

Robert stood over her, resisted the urge to hit her.

"I'm nothing like you. You're a bloody thief Laura, a common thief who has gone into someone's house, seen something you want and just taken it. However, you try and spin it, you stole it. What I want to know is why, I've always given you money, bought you things when you wanted them."

"Oh, the generous, saintly Robert, giving me money. Ask yourself where that money came from, stolen, calling me a thief is rich, you're a lot worse than me. I think you'll find insider share dealing is just as illegal as pocketing some little statue, from a fat slob who beats up women, and spends his weekend with a bunch of prostitutes high on drugs."

Robert turned away from her and walked towards his records. He knew he needed to calm down, but he was finding it difficult to knowing that she had, for some reason, stuck her nose into his business. He spoke to her while looking at his record collection; maybe it was the only thing he truly loved in life.

"I do not steal; I take advantage of the market. The knowledge I have gives me an edge, it makes me a better player."

"It's still fucking illegal," Laura shouted from behind him.

"It's only illegal because the financial institutes need to ensure the wider public think they are honest and above board," Robert now sounded calmer, even though he felt far from calm. "All share dealers tease information from wherever they can. Just to keep up appearances the powers that be have to convict a few people for insider dealing. Gerald only got stung because his vindictive ex-wife informed on him; the FIA had to act. But stealing something like you did, and trying to blackmail someone into doing something, that is a real crime. So, you are going to have to give it back to shut him up."

"I told you, I need it, because I'm leaving you."

Robert turned around to look at her, she was now standing, yet to him she looked unsteady on her feet. She must have been drinking.

"Leaving me, don't be so stupid, who would take on a common little thief like you? No wait, why should I care. Yes, maybe the best thing would be for you to piss off and let me carry on with my life. I pity the poor bastard who takes you on. Gerald will still come after you and I'll be able to wash my hands of you."

"Well, I can, at last, do something right in your bitter and twisted eyes. You've never really loved me, just wanted me around adding to the decoration in the house. A bit of glamour. The only thing you've ever loved is your stupid record collection and telling everyone what a martyr you were to look after your ageing mother. How you cooked and washed for her, such a good little boy. You're not the only one to have to make sacrifices for parents, lots of people do. You're nothing special, just a bent official, the son of a bent accountant who topped himself when he was caught fiddling......"

Robert stopped her speaking, with a firm, open palm which he slapped against her cheek, he did not want to hear any more toxic words from her. She fell onto the floor, her arms and legs juddering and shaking.

"Get up, get your stuff and get out of my life!" Robert walked away, back into the kitchen leaving her on the floor, alone.

Robert poured himself an orange juice, and quaffed it down in one go to sate the thirst his anger had given him. He looked at the photograph attached to the fridge door, it was Laura and himself in Beziers, outside of the arena, a selfie of the two of them enjoying life. He thought he knew her, a bit of a geek, loving old stuff and wanting to enjoy herself. He never imagined, at any time, she might become a sordid, little thief. He would miss her; he also knew he could never trust her again.

He pulled the photograph from the fridge, crushed it in his hands and threw it into the pedal bin.

He walked back to see if she had got up, she was still lying there.

"Stop play acting, just get up and do your packing."

He stepped over her and carefully placed a Simply Red record on the deck, he hated a silent house. As Mick Hucknall's voice echoed across the room, Robert looked at Laura still lying on the floor. He noticed the wet patch around her trousers. Had she been that drunk she had passed out. Robert stared at her for just a few seconds, he was unsure, she had sounded a little drunk, maybe she had taken some sort of drug. He was no longer sure whether he really knew her anymore.

He knelt beside her and shook her, called her name, her jaw fell open. Robert toppled backwards onto his bottom. Sitting on the floor next to Laura, he realised she was not breathing.

Robert began to lose track of time as he sat beside her. 'I've killed her, I've killed her' he recited in his mind repeatedly. As the panic eased from his muscles, he decided to call for help. He pressed nine on his phone twice before stopping.

Without the panic clouding his mind, Robert began to think about the consequences of his action. It had not been his intention to kill Laura, so the charge could only be manslaughter. He would, no doubt, need to serve a custodial sentence. Even if the civil service found him a job when he was released, they would let him nowhere near his current department. He could no longer earn a significant second income. There was another danger. Maybe once he was convicted, they might, as a routine, look back on his work and what he had been doing. He had covered his tracks as best he could but, there was always going to be a but. They might link some innocent conversation or coincidence which might connect him to insider dealing. More time inside. They would certainly sack him for that. The civil service could cope with a killer on its books, but dishonesty where money was concerned, that would be a whole different ball game.

He faced a choice: call the police and risk everything, or take decisive action to deal with the situation and cover his tracks.

* * *

He wished that Laura had bought a bigger car. The Fiat 500 was a sweet car, she liked the Italian styling of the body, the compact size for parking and the very economical engine. The boot just was not big enough for her body. Robert lugged her onto the back seat and covered her with a dust sheet from the garage. It was well past midnight; time was no longer something he was tracking. He just needed to get this done. He hoped, as he drove down the M2, that he would not be the victim of some random police stop.

Birchington was his chosen destination. He recalled from his childhood playing on the rocks and scrambling in and out of the caves. Now, he could see they would present a useful place to stash a body. As he drove, he pictured in his mind, parking on Sea Road. A quiet place at the best of times, so in the early hours of the morning, there should be no one around to observe him as he planned to carry her down the steps, across some rocks and into a cave. That was not going to be easy, she was not a big person, but he had found it difficult enough getting her limp body into the car. As he drove, Robert thought of something that would scupper his plans, he should have checked the tide table first. He prayed it was at least an hour either side of high tide, otherwise his first plan to cover his tracks would fall flat.

Once inside the cave, he planned to stuff as many rocks and stones as he could into her clothing, so that she would be held in place as the tide flooded in, saturating her body every twelve hours. Aided by the crabs and shrimps, that would see her as a feast, her body would soon be difficult to identify.

He made sure he used as many of the main roads as possible, ensuring the automatic number plate recognition cameras tracked the car's journey. He had already turned her phone off, suggesting that she did not want to be tracked. He now wanted to lay a trail away from Sidcup. He knew that once off the motorway, he would disappear from being tracked.

Robert had also taken the opportunity to search her, her clothes and her handbag, as well as her car for any sign of the figurine, and, more importantly, the letter that she had stumbled across. The letter that had incriminated Robert, he would need to be more careful in future. He knew he had mislaid it, he just assumed that he had gathered it up in some papers and it was now either stashed in the spare room or in the recycling bin. In the end, he must have dropped it as he left the house. He needed to be more careful, he reminded himself, especially now as he tried to cover up Laura's death.

If there was a patron saint of murderers, then they were looking after Robert. The tide was far out, and the rocks were reasonably dry. The streets were deserted. It was about two o' clock in the morning when a breathless Robert got back into his deceased partner's car. He stopped on the way to the railway station, took her phone out of her bag, he wanted to use that later. He then dumped her handbag and the dust sheet in the first large industrial waste bin he spotted. Then he arrived at the station, where he planned to park her car. He stepped out into the cold night air and walked across towards the cash machine, he wanted cash to get a cab back. He also wanted the phone, he planned, while driving back in the cab, to turn it on, just for a few minutes, giving support to the scenario that he was trying to compose, that she had been picked up and driven away by her lover, whoever he might be.

He stopped before he was anywhere near the cash machine, the patron saint of murderers seemed to point out, 'Your card, being used to withdraw cash from the station where her car was parked, that would be a vital piece of evidence,' Robert agreed. He needed her handbag. He returned to the car, left the car park and retraced his steps. With a broken branch he fished the handbag out of the rubbish bin, took out her credit cards and left. Once again he drove back to the station car park.

He sat in the car, concerned that he was forgetting the obvious, making possible mistakes. He now needed her PIN number. He was not sure what her number was, they had never shared such information, which had been Robert's idea, he did not want her to be able to check his bank balance or see inside his bank account. Fortunately, his patron saint had guided him to have her phone in his hand. He switched it on, it had to be there somewhere, he had seen her use the phone to remind herself. He looked at her address book, the entry under Card HSBC was a simple 5849. He had it.

He walked out of the station with her credit cards, her phone and one hundred pounds of her money. The next stage was the forty-minute walk towards Westgate-on-Sea and one of the mini-cab companies he knew were located there, as well as dumping the credit cards along the way.

CHAPTER ELEVEN THURSDAY AFTERNOON

The cave was murky, as dark as night and as cold as ice, the air was damp. All Caroline could see was a shadowy figure, crouched in the corner, a small pocket torch drifting over a pile of wet rags. She stood just inside the entrance; her head bent down slightly to accommodate the lack of headroom in the cavern. She watched the light move around, it had to be Robert in there. She could not make out exactly his features or what he was doing but he seemed to be rearranging the rags. Slowly her eyes became accustomed to the darkness, the scene became clearer. She screamed. Her racket echoed around the cave. Robert turned and shone the torch in her face.

"Caroline?"

She did not answer, all she could do was stare at the shadowy face, illuminated by the reflected daylight. It projected out of the pile of wet clothes. A lifeless face. The eyes were no more than black, empty sockets, the cheeks bloated with crinkled skin, hair wet, the mouth open. Beyond the disfigurement, Caroline could recognise the lifeless body that had once contained the living soul of Laura.

She sank to the floor and wept, intense angry sobs that tore at her throat. She felt Robert grab her arms, he pulled her to her feet and shook her.

"Shut up, you stupid bitch, people will hear you."

She did not hear his words, the sound of her sobs filled her head, her tears cascaded down her cheeks. Her fists tried to pummel Robert. He had killed her. He had killed Laura, the only woman she had ever loved.

Her sobs receded; her body numbed. She could only stare at the decaying form of Laura, wishing and praying, that by some miracle she knew could never arrive, Laura would live again.

"Why?" was all she could manage to say. Robert still tightly held her arms.

"I never meant to, it just happened."

She only half listened as he explained what had occurred last week when he returned from the conference. He told her it had been a simple argument and she had fallen. He had panicked and decided to conceal her body.

Caroline's mind was confused and disrupted; she could not think straight. She wanted a strong drink. She wanted to walk out of the cave. She wanted all this to have never happened.

"We need to get help, call the police, Robert, they will help."

He pushed her down onto the wet floor, he turned off the torch. She looked at him, half his face in shadow, half in sunlight. He looked evil, he was, she thought, evil.

"They will be of no help at all, they will only arrest us both and when I tell them about how you helped me, you'll be charged with murder as well."

"I never helped you."

"Well, that will be your word against mine. I doubt if they would have much sympathy for you, when I tell them how we killed her last week and you came to my house and we made love. If I am going to get charged with murder, I'm damn sure I'll take you down with me. Therefore, you had best calm down and help me."

"You're lying, I can prove it."

"Once you're in the hands of the courts, the legal system can be very unforgiving. Is that a risk you're willing to take, I doubt you are?"

She tried to shake off his gripping arms, her movements had no effect, he still held her tight.

"What are you doing here anyway? Or are you such a sick bastard you just wanted to see her dead again." The rebellious Caroline was now starting to emerge from the hysteria she had shown before. Caroline felt she had taken back control of her emotions.

Robert turned and looked at Laura's body, as he did, his face fell into shadow, but for a slight reflection on his eyes.

"Searching for that bloody statue, it's nowhere in my house. I wondered if I might have missed it when I moved her, maybe it was on her all the time. I wanted to find it, give it to whoever wanted it and stop people looking for her. Forget Laura and move on."

"Robert, do you actually comprehend what you have done, you're a murderer! I can't just walk out and forget what I've seen. I loved Laura, you killed her, and I am going to do everything in my power to get her justice."

Robert looked into her eyes; his hands felt like a vice on her shivering arms.

"Do you really think I don't know what I have done. I never planned to kill her; it was an accident. But I am still responsible for her death and the law will still pursue me once they find the body. Maybe they never will, if nature does her work well, then there will just be bones. In time, they might well be washed away. I might get really lucky and some fault in the roof, brings the whole cave down, entombing her forever. Then there will be nothing that will connect me with her death. Or maybe there will. For the rest of my life, I will be looking over my shoulder, sleeping with one eye open, dreading the knock on the door, and seeing a policeman standing there. I would never survive prison."

He stopped talking and stared at Caroline. She soon found out what was going through his mind.

"I took a lot of trouble to bring her here, let the evidence rot away. Now, I am holding another piece of evidence, another link to what I have done. Thankfully, you have come to the very place I would have brought you to, anyway. Thanks for making it easy Caroline. You were the only person in the world who knew what I have done."

His use of the past tense did nothing to allay Caroline's fear. His strong hands moved up from her arms to encircle her fragile throat, thumbs pushing against her windpipe, closing it down, shutting off her life-giving oxygen.

Caroline gasped for air, his body rested against her legs pressing her tight against the floor and leaving her unable to kick out, all she had left were her arms and fists, she tried as best she could to hit and punch him. She was making little difference to his resolve to kill her.

She started to wriggle her body, anything to loosen the grip he had on her throat. Nothing helped. Stars began to fill her eyes; she could make little sound. She feared death at any time, she always had. But here in the dankness of a chalk cave, it seemed to make the transition to death more sordid.

The lack of oxygen now began to spread through her body, her muscles weakened, her already futile resistance was waning further, her organs began the process of shutting down.

* * *

Henry would be the first to describe himself as a bad man, a rum character, someone you would not choose to mess with. He liked that. It gave him influence over the people he encountered. Yet for all his bad traits, Henry had old fashioned standards and morals. He could not understand why people were gay, he could never imagine loving a man, the thought made him shudder. He had a distrust of anyone who had not been born in England, which gave the impression to others that he was a racist. Although he was undeniably racist, when questioned Henry took it further, he distrusted anyone who was not born in London. Everyone else, in his opinion, spoke funny and ate funny food.

Henry would punch a man to death without thinking about it, but he would never hit a woman. It was just not the 'done thing'. As he stepped inside the cave and saw a man throttling a woman, Henry was not pleased.

He instantly pulled the revolver from his waistband, pushed it against Robert's head and said simply,

"Oi, let the girl go, or else your brain will be splashed all over them walls."

Henry held the gun firmly, his finger poised on the trigger ready to shoot. Should Robert move a centimetre in the wrong direction, Henry would not hesitate to kill the man in front of him. Sensibly, Henry thought, Robert released Caroline and moved away.

The sound of release came from Caroline's mouth as she dragged much needed air into her starved lungs. Henry looked around the darkness, he tried to make sense of what was around him. The girl, the man, and in the corner, what looked like a dead woman.

"Who's the stiff in the corner?" He flicked the gun in the direction of the body, just to make it clear what he was talking about.

"Laura," Caroline told him. She was still breathless, sounding as though she had run a hard one hundred metre sprint to win a gold medal. "She was selling," intake of breath, "something to your," another breath, "boss."

"Right, you," he pointed to Caroline, "join him, and put these on, one cuff each."

He handed Caroline the pair of handcuffs that he had taken from his pocket. He watched as Caroline attached one to her wrist and the other to Robert, they were now joined. Henry moved cautiously towards them to check the manacles were firmly fixed to his captives. Now, further inside the cave, Henry was able to stand up, his head almost touching the roof of the chalky grotto.

Henry retrieved his mobile phone from his deep pocket, no signal. He took two steps back, still there was no connection to the outside world. He bent down a little, moved backwards, closer to the entrance.

"Just stay right where you are, don't try anything, I'm happy to kill both of you if I have to," he threatened. Killing a woman was different to hitting a woman in his slightly jumbled mind.

He was now crouched down lower at the entrance to the cave. Squatting down he had a good signal and could still watch his prisoners. He spoke to the phone,

"Hey Google, call Mr Mullins."

The mobile phone replied, "Calling Mr Mullins."

He listened to the ringing; it was answered quickly.

"Mr Mullins, it's me, Henry."

* * *

It was not often that Howard Mullins smiled, yet every time Henry called him, he did. 'Yes,' he thought, 'I know it's you calling, Henry, I can see it on my phone screen'. Henry still had not quite grasped the concept of caller I.D.

"Good to hear from you, Henry. How are things going?"

"Ah, a little mixed up Sir. I'm in a sort of cave place just off Sea Road, the other side of Birchington from your place.

174

Caroline is here, plus some other guy. I'm pretty sure he was with her when she came to see us. It was him who was trying to strangle her, and there is the statue lady, but she's dead."

"Did you kill her?"

"Oh no, Mr Mullins," Henry was quick to reply, "she was already dead, and by the looks of her, dead awhile. Not sure who killed her, do I need to find out?"

"Well, not just yet. Is there any sign of the small statue that the other lady was selling to me?"

Henry asked his two captives if they had the statue? Both denied having it, information he proudly communicated to Mr Howard Mullins. A reply that Howard did not want to hear, it had to be somewhere. Maybe one or both were lying. He would need Henry to put some pressure on them to reveal exactly what they might know. From Henry's description, the current location was not the best place to conduct such a meaningful interrogation.

"Well, I think it is fortuitous that you are close to my weekend retreat. Can you take both our guests there? Make sure they are entertained in the basement and ensure they stay until I get there. I may be a couple of hours or so. Just ensure that there are no shenanigans on the way. Have I made myself clear?"

Howard ended the call with Henry and turned towards Thomas who still sat at the table. Thomas was wearing an anxious face. Howard looked at him and said,

"Well the problem, or should I say your problem, has not exactly gone away, has it, Thomas? I am still substantially out of pocket. Plus, the location of the little figure is currently unknown. You might have gathered from the conversation that things have become a little complex. Our sweet, devious Laura is dead, killed, I would guess, by either her male lover or her female lover, it makes little difference." Howard paused briefly; he saw the reaction on the face of Thomas. The reality of Laura not coming back clearly shocked and saddened Thomas. Howard was not the emotional type, so he just carried on regardless.

"I just need to locate that valuable little toy she was selling. My first question is to you, Thomas, I know you have told me on countless occasions that you do not know the whereabouts of the statue. I assume, and sincerely hope, you are being truthful but, if not, I would suggest that now would be a very good time to disclose any information that you might have."

"I have told you time and time again, I have no idea whatsoever. But let's not forget, the little statue was stolen from one of my very good customers, so strictly speaking, he still owns it."

"You really must try to be a little more dishonest, Thomas. If your drug addict friend starts to claim ownership, I would point out to him that I paid Laura for it, so it is mine in law. He needs to speak to Laura who no doubt has been cheating him. I would also hint that that is the perfect motive for murder."

"Come on, Howard, that's not going to stand up in a court of law."

"Thomas, you really must start to understand that I am referring to the law of the jungle, street law, the rules and regulations that we have to live by, as we work and trade outside of those laws laid down by the establishment. Having said all that, I would be more than happy, should - what was his name, Gerald?"

Thomas nodded.

"I am more than happy to let the police know that Gerald is a likely candidate for murder. Should Laura ever be found that is, no point stirring things up unless you need to. Which leads me onto our arrangement and the substantial amount of money you still owe me."

Howard smugly watched as Thomas moved uncomfortably in his chair, this, he had no doubt, was the moment that Thomas had been dreading, and so he should. He had been most charitable, he thought, providing a substantial amount of money, just so that Thomas could earn himself a quick profit. Not everyone would have been so generous. Howard had, however, misjudged the effect that a pretty girl would have on Thomas, still that was neither here nor there. All Howard wanted was his money or at least some form of repayment.

Howard waited, leaving a silence between them. He wanted an answer from Thomas, a plan of how the debt was going to be paid off.

Thomas made his admission, "I just do not have that sort of money in one payment, I could pay it back over time."

That was precisely the answer that Howard had been hoping to hear. He had already worked out a payment schedule in his head. He just needed to tell Thomas, which was what he was about to do.

"Currently, Thomas, I take five per cent of your profits, an arrangement to thank me for putting up the money for your shop. That will now increase to ninety per cent, a level which will be maintained until your debt and accrued interest is settled in full."

"Ninety per cent! You're having a laugh, Howard; how am I supposed to feed myself?"

"Am I laughing, Thomas? I think not. You have little option."

"This will be ongoing, won't it, there'll be no end date, just me working for you until I die? Maybe I'd be better off dead now, just to spite you."

"My dear Thomas, if you wish, I can arrange that for you. But please, do not think that just by being dead you will spite me. I will still get my money back. The shop, do not forget, belongs to me, I am on the title deeds. Should you happen upon your demise, I will simply put a very cheap worker in there doing exactly what you are doing and still get my money back. You really have little choice."

* * *

It had now been a full week since Sheila had served Laura with her tea. Since that time, Sheila had learnt that Laura had left her home and had not returned, apart from that, she had no other news. Robert had not shared much with her. She was happy with that; the less she knew, the better it would be for her.

She had fully expected that sometime during that Thursday evening, maybe the early hours of Friday morning, she would have heard the two-tone call of an ambulance arriving outside Robert's house, followed by the sound of Medics rushing in, all to no avail. Laura would be dead.

If Sheila was being honest with herself, when she was preparing the Hemlock tea for Laura, she was not exactly sure just how much of a dose to make, as she could not be sure of the toxicity of the plant. All she really wanted was for Laura to die elsewhere, which she had perhaps achieved.

She knew from reading about Socrates, how effective Hemlock could be, as he had committed suicide using the plant. When Sheila first considered killing Laura using Hemlock, it had an irony about it, given that Laura was so immersed in history.

Sheila had spent many hours trawling the internet for information about Hemlock poisoning. The more she read, the more convinced she became it was the right method to use. It was easy to access, and the effects were not immediate, only in time would Laura begin to show the symptoms: burning in her stomach, increased dribbling, rapid heartbeat, trembling, slurred speech, until finally convulsions and death.

You just couldn't kill someone without there being an investigation, Sheila knew that full well. That was why she had kept some teacups from a few days earlier, they would be the ones she would present as the cups used on that Thursday afternoon. She would have, of course, washed them up, but if they needed to be examined forensically, then there would only be innocent traces on the cups. The fatal mugs had long since been disposed of, as had anything that had come into contact with the Hemlock plant.

Sheila was convinced that she had planned a perfect murder, and so far, it had gone better than she had expected. As far as she knew, there was no body to alert the police or anyone else for that matter.

With part one of her plan, which would enable her and Robert to be together, seemingly achieved, now was the time for part two. Her husband needed to die. This afternoon, she was going to make that happen.

Today, the doctor was planning to call in, take some blood, monitor her husband's blood pressure, check his medication. It was just a routine visit, one that occurred every two or three months. Sheila suspected that the doctor found her attractive and was pleased to call as often as possible. She did not mind his attention; in fact, she enjoyed his visits. She was sure he felt for the predicament that she had found herself in. Her husband, who she had to care for constantly, could lie there for another twenty years or just twenty hours. The doctor had said there was no way of knowing. Sheila planned that when the doctor arrived later, her husband would be dead.

She helped her husband climb the stairs towards his bedroom and his regular afternoon sleep, which she had always encouraged. Together, one slow step at a time, they reached the bedroom, where she helped him onto the bed. She took off his shoes and socks, loosened his trousers and removed his cardigan. A routine she knew he recognised and tried his best to help with. Not that he helped, more often he hindered her.

Finally, she pulled the sheet and blanket over him, making sure that he was comfortable.

Last week, as she had placed the Hemlock tea in front of Laura, her heart was racing, fear and adrenaline flowed through her veins. Today, she felt calmer, today, would be so much easier.

She puffed up his pillow, then picked up another pillow.

The internet had informed her that to suffocate someone with a pillow, you needed to apply pressure for about five minutes, after which time the person would be dead.

Sheila lifted herself onto the bed and knelt astride her husband. He looked puzzled.

The plan was to push the pillow hard over his face for at least ten minutes, she wanted to be certain that when the doctor arrived her husband would be dead. She had thought about how she should react when the doctor calls down to her and tells her that her husband must have died in his sleep. Hysteria or calm acceptance? She surmised that his death could be expected at any time, so she would not be surprised. A calm acceptance, with a few tears, maybe a heavy sob, just for effect, should suffice and convince the doctor. He would then be happy to sign the death certificate and she would be able to start her new life with Robert.

"Goodbye, Harold."

She held the pillow in front of her, a hand on each end, her knuckles white, she gripped so tightly. Then there was the first sign of terror in his eyes, as he began in his impaired thinking, to comprehend what she was doing and that what was coming next for him was death.

* * *

"Good afternoon, I'm Detective Constable Hawkins. I am trying to establish the whereabouts of someone we need to interview," Andy lied to the operator at Gary's Cabs. He had often used the same approach, say you're a police officer wanting some, seemingly innocuous, information, which of course would help the police, and the person on the other end of the phone is usually more than happy to help. It had only been on one occasion that the person he was talking to wanted a little more information about him, asking in the end, if they could call the station where he was meant to be based, in order to ensure they were talking to a police officer. At that point, Andy had sensibly hung up.

Today, the man who had answered the telephone at Gary's Cabs was more than happy to help the police. The cab firm was based a couple of miles from Birchington station, the next small town along the coast: Westgate-on-Sea.

"I want to know if you took any cash jobs in the early hours of last Friday morning. I'm only interested in the fare if you had one, nothing else." Andy knew that some cash jobs were, no doubt, never fully recorded, but sometimes businesses are more cautious about the tax man knocking on their door than they are of police officers.

"Hang on, I'll just check," the line went silent as Andy waited. It was not long before Gary's Cabs answered his question, "Yes, here we are, last Friday morning, I was in the office, doing my night shift. Yes, walked into the office, asking for a cab to south London, Sidcup High Street, left here about half three quarter to four, paid cash."

"Sidcup, you say?" Andy was puzzled, why would Laura drive all the way to Birchington in the middle of the night then return to Sidcup. Yes, Andy thought, she really did want to disappear.

"Yes, the bit me and Tony thought queer, Tony was the driver, was the bloke just wanted to be dropped off in the High Street and go the long way round. Guess he needed to creep in quietly, not disturb his missus, I would guess."

"A bloke, you say, not a woman."

"Nah, remember him well, don't get many people just walk in off the street in the middle of the night. Pick-ups from clubs and pubs, but not walk-ins."

"What did he look like?"

"Hard to say, thirty or forty, average sort of height, oh, had odd looking ears. Seemed a nice enough chap though. Not in trouble, is he?"

This changed everything in Andy's mind. It must have been Robert in the cab, he was the one who lived in Sidcup; Gerald, Howard and Thomas lived nowhere near. So, Robert had been at Birchington, had he driven down there with Laura? Why had they gone there? Had they both gone there? Suddenly Andy had too many unanswered questions spinning in his head. One thing was clear, Robert had never mentioned going to Birchington nor getting a cab back. Robert had said that Laura had left about ten pm. Andy recalled that her car was not picked up by cameras until the early hours of the morning. He had assumed she had gone somewhere locally; but maybe she had not. Robert was clearly lying about what he did in the early hours of Friday. If he was lying, then he was covering something up, something bad.

Andy did not have time to work it all out precisely. All he urgently needed to do was warn Caroline, whom he had sent to go and see Robert. He anxiously dialled her number, he needed to alert her, tell her to get out of Robert's house.

* * *

"I honestly never meant to kill her," Robert spoke softly.

Caroline felt his warm breath on her cheeks, 'how can you not mean to kill someone?' she asked herself. She ignored him; she did not want to speak. To speak would mean relaxing some of her taut muscles and they were the only thing stopping her from dissolving into a blubbering mess. Her day had begun by meeting her father, an emotional ride that had instilled some hope that maybe she might find Laura alive and well somewhere after all.

But she had not found Laura; she had only found a shell of the body she had once inhabited during all those good times they had shared.

She tried to resist looking into the dark corner where Laura's body lay wedged, but she had to look again, if for no better reason than to increase her anger towards Robert.

Sitting on the damp, rock floor, handcuffed to Robert, she felt the moisture creeping into her clothes, spreading through the layers that now chilled her skin. She guessed it was the cold, making her shiver, but it could have been the fear of what might happen next. She sat handcuffed to a murderer, and with the silhouette of a man at the entrance to the cave, a gun in his hand, neither were helping her to calm.

Had she happened across Laura's body twenty-four hours ago, she would have happily faced death and taken whatever it brought. Her soul mate was dead, there was no need to continue living. Yet now, she had someone else in her life that she wanted to love, her father. If she was going to die today, then how cruel would that be. Her father would have seen just the smallest glimpse of the daughter he had not seen for many years. Would he even hear that she had died? Her mother had not contacted her father in years. What would he think, his daughter took one look at him, found out he was gay, and never crossed his threshold again? She wondered how he would react, what it might do to him? Henry interrupted her thoughts.

"Do either of you have that statue thing Mr Mullins was buying?"

What a stupid question, Caroline thought, that bloody thing was the cause of all this. Laura seeing it one fateful day and becoming obsessed with it and what it could do for her, the money it could bring in. As it turned out, it was more of a curse. If I knew where it was, I would break it in two.

With two negative answers, Henry continued his conversation.

"I'm sorry," Robert told Caroline. She did not want to listen to his regret. She wanted Laura back.

"I told her it was a bad idea, moving in with you," Caroline admitted.

"I thought she loved me, I loved her. Maybe she loved herself more than she could love others."

"I don't think she loved you in the beginning," Caroline spoke quietly, "but recently I could not be sure. I now know she kept so much hidden from me, and from you. Did either of us really know her?" She turned her head to look at Robert's face, most of which was in darkness, only his eyes were glinting in the shadows, reflecting the sparse sunlight that was entering the cave. "Why here Robert, why did you put her at the back of a cave that it would seem, looking at the walls, fills up at every high tide?"

"I had a dead body in my house, I had never been in that situation, and I guess I panicked. I knew about these caves, having spent a lot of my childhood around this area. I thought that if I wedged and weighed her body down enough, she would stay here, and with the saltwater and the creatures that inhabit these caves, her body would soon be unrecognisable. Evidence would be washed away with the tide."

"God, you're sick, you are happy for her to be eaten up, just to protect you. It sounds like you thought it through well, in your, so-called, panic. Then you come back, just to see if you can find that awful statue. It is cursed you know."

"Don't be stupid."

"Stupid am I. The only reason you came back here was for that thing. By doing so, there are now three people in here, all aware that at the back of the cave is a body. Maybe you would have got away with murdering Laura if you had not been tempted by that ancient carving."

"Shut up you two," Henry interrupted them. "Right, listen carefully," he waved the gun again, to emphasise that he wanted full co-operation. "We are all going to walk out of here, back to my car. Then I'm going to take you to see Mr Mullins, he wants a little chat with you two. So, nothing looks out of place, I want you two to hold hands, just like a couple of lovers walking hand in hand. If we see someone, rest assured that you might not be able to see my gun, but my gun will be able to see you both. Understood?"

"And the choice is?" Caroline asked, she felt Robert preparing to lift himself up from the floor.

"There is no choice young lady, get up and let's get going."

Henry stood at the entrance to the cave and watched as the two of them, hunched over, moved silently towards the sunlight.

The ring tone of a mobile phone echoed out, partly muffled by clothing.

"What's that?" Henry sounded tense.

Caroline answered him, "My phone."

"Give it here."

Caroline, with her free hand, reached into her pocket, the ringing became louder as she held it in her hand. She did not think about it much, she just instinctively threw the phone at Henry. He deflected it away with the hand in which he held the gun, but it was enough to put him off his balance. His foot slipped on the uneven, slippery chalk and he tumbled down awkwardly amongst the uneven rocks.

"Come on," Caroline yanked at Robert, pulling him into action. Quickly passing Henry scrambling on the floor, they dashed out of the cave into the daylight.

* * *

Hearing Caroline's voicemail message did nothing to calm the anxiety that Andy was feeling. What should he do now? He had no idea. Doing nothing was not going to be an option, so phoning Robert's house was next, at least that was something. No reply, just the answer machine. He had to get to the house, then he stopped. Where was Caroline's mobile phone now? His puzzle-solving logic was starting to slip into gear to help him. He checked his computer.

Tower BTS ID273 was the last tower that her phone had connected with, only moments ago, when he had tried calling her. The tower's address chilled him, Canterbury Road, Birchington-on Sea. Once again, the coastal village of Birchington had surfaced, the location where Laura's car had been found. This only increased his anxiety. He had to get there, it was a long drive, at least ninety minutes from his office in London, but what other options did he have. There was no guarantee that if he kept calling, she would answer.

What could he tell the local police? He had little to go on. He could get there and find Caroline and Robert chatting happily in a restaurant. But deep in his heart he knew that Caroline was in danger.

He grabbed his coat and laptop and called to a colleague telling him that he would be back when he got back.

Mid-afternoon and the city traffic was light. Within fifteen minutes he was joining the coastbound A2, driving as fast as he could, as fast as the traffic would allow him to. His mind whirled over the possible different scenarios ahead of him. He needed information. He called hands-free back to his office.

"Peter, it's me."

"Where did you dash off to?"

"No questions, Peter, there's no time. Listen, I need a favour, that girl who joined us in the pub yesterday, I think she needs help and I need to find her urgently. I want you to triangulate her phone so that I can get as close as I can to where her phone is."

"Sounds exciting, what's her number?"

As Andy gave him the number, he saw two flashes in his mirror in quick succession, a speed camera. No doubt the first but not the last speeding ticket of the day, he thought.

"Call me back when you have it. Make it top priority, no beer breaks till you've found her."

"I'm on the case."

"Just one other thing, let me know where Robert's phone is."

"Robert, our Rob you mean?"

"Yes, no questions please, just do it."

Andy cut the connection and focussed on his driving. Now he was moving away from the London streets, the overtaking was easier. He just hoped the speeding ticket was going to be worth it.

* * *

The wind was strong and gusty, as well as being very cold, whipping the rain into piercing shards that stung Caroline's face. She moved as fast as she could, but not as fast as she wanted to, over the slippery ice-like rocks with Robert, still firmly connected to her, doing his best to help the two of them keep their balance.

Running was not an option in this rugged environment. The craggy stones, rocks and small pools of water made a quick dash to the road impossible. She knew that it would take a moment or two for Henry to get up, he would see them moving away. She just hoped that he did not decide just to let off a volley of gunfire.

She banked on the fact that such an action would draw attention to them all. Someone would be bound to call the police.

Caroline had no plans to look back and see where Henry was, that would only delay their escape.

"Over to the right, there are some more steps, do you see them?" Robert called her through the wind, pointing with his free hand.

She saw the steps, they had to be their best option. She changed her tack and tried to navigate as best she could, struggling to find the path of least resistance. The rocks, uneven, wet, oily, hindered them at every step. At least they would also hinder Henry, Caroline thought, but he had the advantage of being on his own, whereas they were shackled together. Henry also had the gun.

Using hands and feet, like four-legged creatures, they scrambled more than ran, stumbled more than walked, faced being captured more than being able to escape. Caroline heard Henry's shouts grow closer. Could they hide? Caroline was not sure; all she knew was that being handcuffed to Robert was a hinderance they could both do without.

She heard a loud profanity from Henry, she turned and saw he had stumbled and was trying to drag himself up from between two rounded lumps of rock. This was an opportunity to change tack.

"This way," Caroline tugged Robert left, away from the direction they had been travelling. She had seen three large formations of rock a short struggle away. She pulled Robert down in between the rocks, out of sight of Henry, she hoped. They squatted, regaining their breath, their clothes soaking wet from the rain and the rock pools they had trodden through.

Above the sound of the wind they heard Henry shout out, frustration in his voice, "Where the fuck are you? Bloody troublemakers, I'll find yer sooner or later."

Caroline had gambled, would they evade him, or would he find them? She looked at Robert's frightened eyes. If only she had a gun, she would kill him first and Henry second.

* * *

Mentally, Andy ticked off the landmarks as he passed them: under the M25, Bluewater exit, Medway Bridge, past Medway services, Isle of Sheppey turn off. Maybe another half an hour and he would be close to Caroline or at least her phone. His phone rang.

"Andy, good news and bad news."

Andy did not want to hear any bad news from the hands-free speaker. It was bad enough the rain had started and was gaining strength with every mile he travelled. The windscreen wipers were working as hard as they could. The spray from the vehicles around him were inhibiting his vison and slowing him down.

Peter continued, "Robert's phone last showed around his home address earlier today. It is now off and has been for a while. The other number, the girl's number."

"Caroline," Andy added.

"Caroline's number, last signal was thirty minutes ago, bounced off two towers, BTS ID 988..."

Andy interrupted, "Give me a road not a sodding tower, I need a road."

"Sorry, Epple Bay Avenue and Sea Road, that's the area you need to aim for; can't get any closer than that."

"What did you mean last signal?"

"I mean her phone is now off-line, nothing from it at all."

"Shit!" Andy did not mean to say that out loud, he only meant to think it. He had spoken out of the frustration he was feeling, as well as his rising guilt for asking Caroline to do a favour for him, to just pop in and see Robert.

"Is there anything else I can do?" Peter asked.

"Sorry, Peter thanks, nothing at the moment, I'll get back to you if I do."

The rain continued, the spray from the traffic around him intensified. Andy feared the worst and pushed his right foot down further, driving faster than he knew he could safely go. For the first time in years he prayed.

* * *

"Look, I just want to take you back to see Mr Mullins. We ain't gonna hurt yer," Henry shouted across the shoreline. "I'm getting bloody wet, which I hate. So just stand up and we'll all go and get ourselves dried off."

Caroline tried to judge how close he might be to them. It was hard to tell without peeking over the top of their hiding place and that was too much of a risk for her.

Robert whispered close to her ear, "let's stand up, maybe we'll have a better chance away from the beach, it's not the best place to run, is it?"

"Don't be so stupid, Robert, this is our only chance. We take it, or I'd not like to think what comes next."

"Mr Mullins only wants the statue," Henry called out once more, this time his voice seemed to be further away. Caroline imagined him moving between the rocks, looking into the crevices, gun in hand.

"I never meant to kill her, I honestly didn't," Robert pleaded with Caroline.

"This is not the time or place," Caroline spoke with a hushed, irritated voice, she did not want her words carried on the wind to Henry's ears. "There'll be time enough for you to explain to the police once we are away from here. Just stop talking and wait. That bloke will tire soon enough."

Caroline did not really believe that Henry would grow tired of his search. She guessed that Henry was a faithful pet to Mr Mullins and would keep poking around the shore until he found them. She also realised that the tide was coming in. The hiding place that Robert and she cowered in would soon be under water.

She listened as Henry continued to talk to them, reasoning that it would be for the best if they gave themselves up to him. The volume of his voice rose and fell as he moved around, sometimes closer, sometimes further away. It was as if he was trying, by letting them know where he was, to scare them out of their cover if he got too close. Caroline resolved to stay put, her heart racing as Henry's voice grew louder.

"Mr Mullins won't mind if you've killed someone."

Caroline sensed he was getting even closer to them.

"I think he respects killers in a funny sort of way."

Closer still.

"Mr Mullins has always been kind to me."

Yet closer.

Caroline hoped her breathing could not be heard above the wind and the falling rain. She fought the intense urge to lift her head higher and look around.

"There you are."

Caroline looked up to see Henry standing above them, looking down with a smug look on his face as his coat flapped in the wind and he swayed slightly to resist the force of it.

"Now be a good boy and girl and come along nicely this time. I could just shoot you here," he helpfully pointed out, "but as

I told yer before, Mr Mullins wants a word. So, get up and we'll go back to my warm car."

Robert and Caroline stood up the best way they could in the narrow crevice, still unsteady on the wet stone. Next, they needed to clamber up to where Henry stood.

"Give us a hand up, it's bad enough on the seaweed, let alone being attached to him," there was venom in her voice. She offered her hand to Henry, who squatted down and grabbed it. Without any hesitation, she pulled hard on his hand, his feet slipped, and he tumbled down beside her.

"Run!"

She pushed a surprised Robert to his left and along a narrow gap, which gave them a better route away from a blaspheming Henry, who was desperately trying to get up. Out of the shelter of the rocks they were once again fighting the gusty wind and driving rain. They had another chance to escape.

* * *

Andy left the motorway and joined the Thanet Way; the rain had eased a little. With less traffic he could now drive faster. Already he knew he had passed three speed cameras, each one catching him breaking the speed limit, that would mean at least nine points on his licence. He wondered if he could offer up mitigating circumstances as a reason and hoped there would be no more cameras along the route. The next one could mean a driving ban.

Along the motorway between manoeuvres, he had put Sea Road, Birchington into his Sat Nav, that would be his starting point. Why had he not seen the connection between Laura and Caroline, even with hindsight their relationship surprised him. If he was honest, he always fancied his chances with Laura after she had moved in with Caroline. It was Robert who had beaten him to it. Looking back, he now had several regrets, not dating Laura was one, others included not being more forceful when he knew that she was going to be dealing with criminals, he should have stopped her, asked more questions and insisted that she give him answers.

He also regretted not seeing what was obvious to him when Robert had told everyone that Laura had walked out on him about ten that evening. He could see the first time her car showed up on the ANPR cameras was in the early hours of the following morning. He had just assumed that she had gone somewhere locally, without her phone being turned on, but it should have been a big enough clue for him that things were just not right.

"Shit!" Andy called out. He saw the speed camera later than he would have liked. The yellow box on the grey leg was waiting at the side of the road, waiting to trap motorists. Was he going to risk three more points and a full ban? He pushed his foot hard on the brake, he needed to reduce his speed by thirty miles per hour to pass the camera without being snapped. He watched the speedometer drop.

He then felt the rear of the car snake outwards towards the central reservation. He tried to counter the swerve, which became a sideways skid. He pushed harder on the brake. Wrong action, he realised, as the rear of the car whipped sharply around, now facing the oncoming traffic and sliding backwards, heading for the hard shoulder and a grassy embankment.

He had lost control and braced himself for the inevitable impact, which came with a dull, yet loud, thud as the rear of his car stopped instantly against the grass and litter-covered bank. His head was thrown back against the head rest. There was no silence, cold wind rushed into the car, the back window had shattered in the accident. He turned and looked at the glass-strewn back seat, rain falling through the open aperture. He turned back to the front, then watched through the waving windscreen wipers as two cars, hazard lights flashing, approached him, slowing down, coming to his aid. Andy did not have time for help, he turned the ignition key and prayed for the second time today.

* * *

Once again Caroline found herself cursing the burden of Robert beside her as she struggled over the ever-growing rocks and stones that formed the foreshore. The steps, leading up to the road, were getting closer, as was Henry. She glanced over her shoulder and saw that he had regained his feet and was, once more, back in pursuit of them.

The route that she could make out ahead of her was over a selection of medium-sized rocks, that would take them first to the left of the steps and then back towards them. There was an alternative way, a direct path, that would take her and Robert over a very tall mound of stone; a Goliath of an outcrop, which was by far the shortest but not the easiest way of getting to the steps. Apart from the shelter of the slab, the two of them would be a clear target for Henry should he decide that letting off a few bullets in their direction might put a quick and easy end to the chase, but she had to chance it

"This way," she pulled hard on the handcuff, leading Robert as if he was a badly behaved dog out for its walk. "Over the top of that one and we should be home and dry," she tried to sound optimistic.

They began to climb the rock as if it was a mountain to be conquered. No more than fifteen feet high, they were able to find the odd foot and hand hold as they scaled upwards. By now they seemed to have found a rhythm and understanding. Robert allowed

194

his manacled hand to be guided by Caroline, then the rest of his body followed, their progress was getting easier.

Caroline did not hear it; the wind was still deafening. She saw a lump of stone which seemed to eject itself just a foot or two away from her, dust and splinters rose up and were washed away in the wind. A bullet. Henry had ramped up the ante. He had made it clear to Caroline and Robert that he was not going to mess around anymore.

She reached the top, Robert, his feet still slipping, was struggling to get alongside her. Another splinter of rock flew up beside Robert, the bullet bounced away from them. The surprise was enough for Robert to lose the secure footing he had just found, only his free hand was left to hold him. It was not enough, the wetness conspired against him, and he began to slide downwards. As much as she tried, Caroline could not hold on with his weight dragging her down. The slide became a fall, a rolling tumble over the uneven glossy barnacle covered rocks. Then, nothing, as they fell through space, only a few feet. She rolled crashing into Robert, pushing him down into a narrow crevice where they landed, she on top of Robert.

"Get up, Robert, get up, for Christ's sake!" She knew she almost screamed, she was not proud, but she could no longer contain the fear within her and the realisation that her gamble might not have paid off, Henry would soon be upon them.

They had landed wedged together between two large granite slabs, that had been weathered by the tides over the centuries.

Caroline was pressed up close against Robert. She realised, apart from being almost entangled, they were lying in the remains of a small rock pool, a crab scuttled away. Then she saw the water change colour to a light pink which was growing darker and darker. She turned her head as best she could. Robert was not moving. His head was an open wound, cracked open as if it had been an egg. She retched, turned her head away and tried to think of an escape, a way of breaking the manacle that now held her firmly to a comatose body.

She pulled as hard as she could, willing her wrist to slip through the handcuff. She was only succeeding in tearing her skin and adding more blood to the rock pool.

"Oh dear," the voice was panting heavily. Caroline looked up and saw Henry, silhouetted against the grey sky. "Looks like you got yourself in a right pickle, Miss, and he don't look too clever now, does he?"

"Do you want to help me get out of this mess?" Caroline asked, looking up at Henry.

She could not make out his face, but she did see him raise his arm and point a revolver at her.

* * *

The engine burst into life. Andy revved it to reassure himself the motor would not fall out, then slipped it into first gear and released the clutch. He put full lock on the steering wheel and swung the entire car around and back onto the Thanet Way towards Birchington. Leaving behind, no doubt, two very surprised drivers, as well as his entire rear bumper and a selection of broken plastic bits which had been his rear light cluster.

He increased his speed, the rain started to diminish, and the road was almost empty. In his door mirror he could see part of the rear wheel arch flapping around, loosened through the coming together with the grassy knoll. He ignored it and continued. He turned off the Thanet Way onto Canterbury Road, just a few miles now before he would be at his destination. Once there, he would need to try and find Caroline, he hoped there might be some clues, something, anything to indicate where she was.

Andy called Peter at the office to ask if Caroline's phone had come back online, the answer was negative, it was the same for Robert's phone, no activity at all. It did not bode well.

Again, he questioned his response. Was he overreacting, was there going to be some innocent reason behind the data he had? Part of him hoped and prayed that one day he might look back on today and laugh about it all. In a few minutes he might have the answer.

* * *

"What are you going to do? Go ahead, shoot me here and get it over with, or do you have to call your boss first?" Caroline waited for an answer or the report of the gun. If this was the end, then she was ready. She might never see her father again, but then, on the plus side, if there is a heaven, she would be with Laura.

"Ah, Miss, I am allowed to make my own decisions. Mr Mullins says that sometimes I need to just do what I think is right. He calls it something clever..." he paused, "dynamic assessment, he calls it."

"So, what do you think is going to happen next?" Even as she spoke, Caroline moved her wrist against the handcuff, rubbing and pulling the skin from it. She tried not to grimace as she attempted, once more, to pull her hand through the manacle.

"Well, I look at it this way; I would love to stay and watch you, through some miracle, drag him out and pull him up the shore to the road. Now, if you did somehow manage that, which I doubt you will, then you're gonna' have to explain just why you have a dead body attached to your wrist. That would make an interesting conversation. Although, I guess you needn't worry too much about what you're gonna' say. In about an hour the tide will be in and you'll be some five or six feet under the surface attached to a dead body, so you ain't gonna' float, are you? The best you can look forward to, I reckon, is drowning. Saves me actually having to shoot you." Henry laughed.

Caroline gritted her teeth, continuing her efforts to pull her wrist out of the handcuff.

"Hate to tell you, but you're buggered, Miss, whichever way you go. I'll say goodbye now, nice knowing you."

"What about that friggin' statue everyone is after? You might never find it if I die here. Unlock these handcuffs, I'll come with you and maybe me and your boss can work things out, find the valuable figure he desires so much."

Henry squatted down, she could now see his face a little easier, he had a worried look.

"That's just it, Miss, that might well be the best option, but I've lost the key to them 'cuffs, so I can't let you go. At least by leaving you here, I can tell Mr Mullins that you both died. I needn't mention I lost the key, that might upset him, and I do try not to upset him. I'll be off now, good luck."

Henry stood up, pushed the pistol into his pocket, turned and disappeared from her view. Caroline wanted to cry but would not allow herself the luxury. As she continued fighting her shackle, she thought about the father she would never see again. She just hoped that once the tide had arrived, she would at least meet up with the only person in her life that she had ever truly loved.

What would Laura say when they were reunited as angels amongst the clouds of heaven: 'You just gave up, you didn't fight, there's always another option.' Caroline guessed that would be Laura's reaction. There had to be something she could do.

She looked once more at Robert, pushed her hand against his neck, she could feel no pulse, his chest was still. If he was dead, he was not going to feel what she was about to do, but even if he was slightly conscious, she didn't really care if he felt pain.

She stretched outwards towards a large stone that, when she picked it up, filled the palm of her hand. She twisted her body to make what she was going to do easier. She moved Robert's hand, so that it was laying on a slab of granite, then brought the stone down with as much force as she could muster. Water splashed up as the stone made impact, but so far it had not done much to the hand. She brought it down again and again. The skin split, blood dripping out into the pool of water she was laying in.

Exhausted as she was, she continued to smash the lifeless hand, harder and harder. The soft flesh becoming a red pulp, muscle and blood mixing. Harder she brought the stone down. The first bone broke, and his index finger came away and floated in the water. It inspired her to continue. She had to break his hand away from the rest of his body, it was the only chance she had of escaping death.

Time was now relevant to her. Pummelling his hand, cracking and breaking bones, she was almost through when she noticed, for the first time, the sea water in her intimate crevice rise then fall. The tide was arriving. Her life clock was now being counted down as the waves began to reach her.

* * *

Anxiously, Andy drove along Epple Bay Avenue then onto Sea Road, looking for anything that might give away just where Caroline and Robert were. He passed the houses along Epple Bay driving cautiously, until he saw ahead of him Robert's car. He accelerated and saw Caroline's car parked a little further on from Robert's. He slid to a halt behind Caroline's car and got out, surveying what was around him.

This part of Sea Road was deserted, on one side was the cliff edge, and on the other an empty golf course. Wind and rain had kept all the golfers firmly at the nineteenth tee. There were houses several hundred yards ahead of him and behind him. He stood in what felt like an empty void, a residential no-man's land.

He looked across the shore, the wind was whipping up the waves as they crashed onto the rocks.

"Caroline," he called as loud as he could manage, his voice suppressed by the wind. Nothing, no clues, no movement, just an empty shore. He looked around him again, this time he noticed steps leading down to the shoreline, one set on his left, one set on his right. He had a choice, would it make any difference, was she even on the shore? At least if he was down there among the rocks, he would be able to see all the shoreline. He chose the right-hand steps and ran towards them.

* * *

Caroline wished she could scream out and someone, anyone, would come to rescue her. There had been no one to see her being shot at. No one had reported gunfire. No one had called the police. She had only herself. She continued to smash Robert's hand, now no more than a red stump, which still would not slip through the handcuff. However hard she hit; it was refusing to let go of the handcuff.

The tide was now firmly around her. Robert's body was semi-submerged, she had to partly kneel up to keep most of her body out of the water. Sea water covered his hand, softening the blows that she rained down on him. With each eddy the tide brought in, it washed away the body debris, cleaned the water sending his amputated fingers out to sea, teasing her to try again, with ever exhausted strikes.

In desperation she started to hammer the wrist. Maybe she could break through that bone, maybe that was where she should have started. How she wished she had paid more attention in her biology classes. All Caroline knew was that she was running out of strength and running out of time.

* * *

The rocks at the bottom of the steps were just as slippery as the steps themselves. Andy held onto the handrail to steady himself. He studied the shoreline; it was a desolate place. Where the tide was coming in, waves crashed onto the rock and the spray was carried on the wind. Not a soul in sight. Not even a hardy fisherman.

He turned his attention to the chalk cliffs. They were not as grand as Dover or the Seven Sisters, just small chalk cliffs, in some places eroded by the tides. He noticed the dark entrances to some caves, he doubted they would be very deep or as complex as other cave systems. His mind turned to Hastings caves, where he had visited as a child. Maybe they were in one of these caves sheltering. He stepped cautiously over the rocks. He could not delay; the tide was coming in and the high-water mark was well above the cave entrances he was looking at.

Thankfully, he thought, the wind had eased, making traversing the shore a lot easier. The rain was still in the air but was more of a light drizzle now. The sound of the incoming tide and the gulls squawking was clearer and were more the sounds he was used to at the coast. He looked to his right at the gulls, Black-headed gulls were fighting with Herring gulls, he noticed even a Sparrowhawk getting in on the act.

He watched as a small Black-headed gull picked something up and lifted off, followed by three Herring gulls harrowing it for the prize in its mouth, which it promptly dropped.

Andy was no more than a hundred feet from their quarrel, he watched as the food dropped. Surely it was not a fish, or anything that looked to be nautical, maybe it was just some bread, but the meat-eating Sparrowhawk was equally interested.

He thought he recognised it, but it seemed too bizarre, he had to be mistaken. A finger, yes, it did look like a finger. He negotiated the uneven route towards the battling birds. As he got closer, a lucky Herring gull grabbed the object and flew away, with three others chasing after it. He then realised that the remaining gulls and the Sparrowhawk assembled at a spot, scavenging around. The wind started to build again.

He moved carefully around a large rock, maybe the biggest on the beach, he wanted to get closer to whatever was interesting the birds so much. It was the only unusual thing he could see on this deserted beach. It could be a waste of time, but he had to be certain. Watching the birds so intently, he stumbled as he trod on what felt like a foot, a man's foot. He looked down to see two people, one submerged, and Caroline, tears flowing from her eyes, sitting up smashing a rock down onto Robert's body.

* * *

Caroline heard her name being called, was this it, was this death taking her? She turned to see Andy. Was he really there or was she just dreaming him? Even if he was death, she would be content to fall asleep and die in his arms.

He pulled her towards him. She felt the welcome warmth of his body.

"You're safe now," was all he said.

She watched through her exhausted and stinging eyes, as Andy pulled his phone out. She listened; she was still unsure that she was not just hallucinating.

"Police, I need help urgently..."

Her confused mind could not take in everything he was saying, she heard "tide coming in" "one body, one alive" "Sea road, Birchington".

Then she felt his arm lift her higher up from the incoming tide that now washed around her waist.

"Help is on its way, Caroline; we'll get through this and you'll be chatting with your dad before you know it."

That was exactly what she wanted to hear; she would see her father again.

EPILOGUE

She had not seen her husband's eyes as close as this since the days they courted. Sheila had always loved his eyes; they were a dark brown with small white flecks in them. When they first dated, she often described them as deep pools of love, pools that she wanted to drown in. During the time of their marriage, she had started taking his eyes for granted. Then over the last few years, she hardly ever looked at them. She avoided looking too closely at her broken husband, it made her uncomfortable to see him impaired.

It seemed strange to her that today as she was straddled across him, a pillow in front of her ready to push it against his face, those eyes once again became her focal point. They were still deep brown in colour but, rising from the pools of love that she once saw them as, all she now saw was terror.

He might have problems communicating, he might shuffle around the house and need to be dressed, undressed, fed, and bathed, he was a large baby that she needed to care for, but he seemed to understand that his wife was about to put an end to his life. He clearly would have no idea as to the reason, he just knew it was going to happen.

Sheila looked into his eyes. She recalled their wedding day, standing in church, speaking her marriage vows out loud, in front of the congregation, in front of God, 'look after him in sickness and in health'. Killing your husband was not in keeping with the vows she had sworn to uphold.

There had been no feeling of guilt in Sheila when she had served Laura poisoned tea, why should there have been, she had made no divine vow of protection for Laura.

Sheila could not kill her husband. Maybe for all his imperfections she still loved him, she was not sure. She threw the pillow to one side and got off the bed, knelt beside him and held his cold hand.

"I'm so sorry, Harold, it was a terrible, terrible thing I was going to do, but I just can't. I love you too much."

That close to the bed she smelt an odour she recognised, urine. There had been nights that he had wet the bed, unable to control his muscles. Today it was through fear. Resigned to be his nurse she set about getting him into a chair and taking the sheets from the bed. Then she removed all his clothes and helped him into his pyjamas. She had at least an hour before the doctor would arrive.

"Let's get you some fresh sheets, Dear. Oh, your spare set is in the wash. I'm afraid it will be the old set, the candy stripes that you always hated, but you've peed the bed so you can't complain, can you?"

She opened the wardrobe where she had stashed all the old out-of-fashion bedding and tugged at a set of striped sheets, then noticed a rucksack. She had never seen it before. Leaving the sheets on the carpeted floor; she extracted the heavy rucksack from the wardrobe and opened it.

She gasped; the mysterious rucksack was stuffed full of bank notes. How much she had no idea; it was more than she had ever seen in her life. From the first handful she pulled out, all twenty-pound notes, she estimated she was holding at least one thousand pounds. She could not imagine how much the whole rucksack contained.

"Harold, where did all this come from?" She wasn't expecting an answer and did not get one. As well as the bank notes, there was a ball of tissue, she unwrapped it to reveal a small beige-coloured figurine.

"Well I'll be jiggered; have you been stashing money away? I suppose it must be ours, it's in our house, it's like a gift from heaven. I'll be able to pay someone to help out. Oh, and this little figure will look lovely lying on the sideboard."

As Sheila pushed her treasure back into the wardrobe before the doctor arrived, she wondered if this was God saying, 'thank you' to her for maintaining her wedding vows.

The End.

AUTHOR NOTES

The story line of a missing partner, who then turns out to have been living a secret life is not new, I'll be the first to admit. So do forgive me.

The idea for this story had been bouncing around in my mind for several years and underwent several revisions, before finally seeing the light of day. Then there is the ever-present conundrum of what to call the book. Inspiration was finally found when listening to a song by a 1980's pop group called ABC. At once I knew that was going to be the title for the book. The full title of the song, 'The Night You Murdered Love' sounded a little too much like a love story, so the shortened version, 'The Night You Murder' fitted the bill, I hope you agree.

Within the story I have taken a few liberties, as all authors do, especially on the coast-line close to Birchington, where Robert found a place to hide the evidence. Don't expect to find any large caves in which you can hide a body, (you'll need to look elsewhere). Andy also was given a few fictional tricks when he was examining Laura's phone records, although it is scary just how much information is out there about our everyday movements.

I would love to hear what you thought of the story, good or bad, as I know I can't please everyone. You can let me know your opinion of the book either via an Amazon or a GoodReads review or simply leave a message on my Facebook page: Adrian Spalding author.

Until the next time.

Sleeping Malice
by Adrian Spalding
'Your past never forgets.'

When journalist Helen Taylor lands her dream job on a newspaper, she could never have imagined that her first assignment would become her worst nightmare.

Travelling to France for a simple story, Helen encounters Phillip, a puzzling Englishman who avoids contact with anyone. When she meets him, she feels there is something dark about him, which may provide her with a major scoop.

Greg, an out-of-work journalist, also arrives in the village asking questions about a missing man. With the appearance of two journalists, one English family fears they are being hunted for the secret they hold.

So when Her Majesty's Government stretches its merciless talons across the English Channel, Helen and Greg have to work together to discover just what has been hidden in the village.

As they begin to uncover the facts, their own suppressed secrets start to emerge. They learn that when your past comes back to haunt you, no one around you is safe.

Available now from Amazon

What readers have said on Amazon about 'Sleeping Malice':

'Rooted in real places, this book takes the reader beyond the believable facade of everyday characters to the darkly sinister, yet utterly logical crimes created in their minds and executed with poker faces.'

'I had no idea where the plot was taking me, the multiple plot lines were all compelling and exciting and this was one of those books I would go to bed early to read!'

The Reluctant Detective
by Adrian Spalding
'A humorous crime mystery.'

Martin never planned to do any actual detecting. He just wanted a quiet life. Something his mother was not going to allow. There again he never for one moment imagined he would have to look into the death of a 90-year-old lady who was gambling away her family fortune.

Soon the Reluctant Detective is grappling with shady estate agents, an intellectual artist, missing charity money and an irritating Indian waiter. Luckily for Martin there is help in the form of Colin, a transvestite who, apart from having very good fashion sense, is an expert at breaking into houses.

Available now from Amazon

What readers have said on Amazon about 'The Reluctant Detective':

'The book is well written and humorous. I enjoyed all the major characters and look forward to reading another story about them. I do hope that Colin and Becky actually join Hayden Investigations.'

'A delightful book that is a real page turner. I want to know what life has in store for the characters of Hayden Investigations and eagerly await the next book in the series.'

'Funny & quirky. Thoroughly enjoyed it & hoping there will be another'

Printed in Poland
by Amazon Fulfillment
Poland Sp. z o.o., Wrocław

56729674R00127